BOUND BY
HELL

ERIN BEDFORD

Bound By Hell © 2018 Embrace the
Fantasy Publishing, LLC

MORE BY ERIN BEDFORD

The Underground Series
Chasing Rabbits
Chasing Cats
Chasing Princes
Chasing Shadows
Chasing Hearts
The Crimes of Alice

Fairy Tale Bad Boys
Hunter
Pirate
Thief
Mirror
Stepbrother

The Mary Wiles Chronicles
Marked By Hell
Bound By Hell
Deceived By Hell
Tempted By Hell

Starcrossed Dragons
Riding Lighting
Grinding Frost
Swallowing Fire
Pounding Earth

BOUND BY HELL

ERIN BEDFORD

1

GRACIE LOU FRANKLIN WAS the very definition of innocent—from the tight dark curls on her head to her big blinking eyes. Even the way she sat in the rickety old chair across from my desk screamed untouched.

But what Gracie Lou had just asked me to do was most definitely not innocent. Not one bit.

"So let me get this straight," I leaned forward in my chair behind my second-hand desk, my hands clasped in front of me, "You want me to summon a demon so that you can get back at your coworkers for making fun of you?"

"Yes." She gave a short nod. The smile on her face should have belonged to a different conversation completely, not for making deals with demons.

"How old are you exactly?"

My question made her smile wilt slightly but within seconds it was back, her eyes crinkling at the edges. "I'm thirty-four."

"Really?"

Being nonhuman myself I was the last person who should be questioning someone's age, but based on my time on earth she did not look even close to the women I'd seen in the over thirties group. Heck, she looked more like she should be going to high school with Trisha. Or at least college.

"See," she pointed her finger at me, the skin on her cheeks pulling tight, "that's my problem right there. No one believes me when I tell them my age. They are constantly torturing me about my youthful features and I'm tired of it. It's their turn to get a taste of their own medicine."

It was about revenge. Revenge I understood. I had my own revenge that needed to be carried out, but even if I understood her motives, I wouldn't kill someone for money.

Even if I needed it.

A few weeks ago, I had ended up in the hospital while hunting down a killer for the LAPD. Not surprisingly, the LAPD hadn't agreed to foot my hospital bills. Which left me with little choice but to take on as many cases as possible to pay the bill off. Hence the woman before me.

I sighed, running a hand through my hair. "Look, I want to help you out. I really do. But it wouldn't be ethical, let alone *legal*, for me to kill someone for money."

"Oh, I don't want you to kill them," Gracie Lou jumped in, her mouth slightly agape at the prospect.

"Then what *do* you want me to do to them?"

She shrugged her tiny shoulders, "Just scare them a bit. Maybe say something like 'this is for messing with a sweet girl like Gracie Lou'. Or something like that." When I raised a brow at her, she gave an irritated sigh, "Here, I can pay you cash." She dug into her purse and pulled out a large stack of bills. My eyes locked onto it, the amount there more than enough to cover this month's expenses. And then some.

But I shook my head. "I'm sorry. Even if I were able to summon a demon for you, I wouldn't."

"Why not?" she whined, her innocent act beginning to wane.

"For one, I *exorcise* demons, not summon them, so, I'd have to figure out how to do that. Two," I held up two fingers, "Demons are not lap dogs you can call at your will. They don't go by our rules—or any rules for that matter. Bringing a demon to this plane is all fine and dandy, but trying to control it once it gets here?" I shook my head, "That's as likely as me sprouting wings and flying."

Gracie Lou's lips poked out in a pout, "But I have all this money," she dug around in the little purse on her shoulder and pulled out a large stack of bills. She sat it on my desk, I knew she was trying to tempt me with the money. But I wasn't like humans. While I needed the money, the sight of the bills piled up before me didn't quite have the same hold on me as it would a normal person. My eyes only briefly landed on the money before going back to Gracie Lou's.

"Some things aren't about money, Miss Franklin. This is about innocent people getting hurt," I stood from my chair and gestured to the door, "Now if you don't mind, I have other clients to see."

Gracie Lou frowned and her eyes narrowed, but got to her feet. She snatched the pile of money off of my desk and shoved it back into her purse, "You're going to be sorry you didn't help me. I'll find someone else to raise my demon."

I shook my head at her, "Only a crazy person would do what *you* are asking."

As an angel, I could read more than people. I could read their souls and Miss Franklin screamed evil. Before she stomped out of my office, I dropped the veil over my powers and stared into her soul. It was mostly pale white but there in the center of her chest was the beginnings of a dark soul. As I'd thought. Gracie Lou might look sweet and innocent but her soul was getting tainted by the minute. It gave me a bad feeling.

I had no doubt she would try to get someone else to raise the demon. I just hoped she didn't try to do it herself.

"Hey Mary, I've got your messages," Trisha, my receptionist-slash-hacker-on-demand, strolled into my office holding up a pile of small papers.

The office was made up of two rooms and a bathroom. The front room served as the waiting area with Trisha's desk off to one side. The other room was my office and bedroom, with the only bathroom lead off it. I had a fold-out couch in there that I slept on. It wasn't much but I liked it.

"Alright," I said as she stopped at my desk and leaned against the edge.

"Don't you want to know what they are?" she waved them at me in a teasing manner.

Shrugging a shoulder, I frowned, "Not really."

"Well, too bad. I'm going to read them to you anyways," she held up one of the papers and started to read, "Bruce Stachler called. Says he thinks his poodle is possessed and wants you to come take care of it."

"Take care of it?" I cocked a brow at her.

"You know," Trisha mimicked holding a shotgun with her hands, and included sound effects.

"Okay," I drew out, not sure exactly how I was going to handle that one. I'd never worked with a possessed animal before. Then again, there was that incident with

13

the horde of pigs running off a hill a few thousand years ago.

"Then there's a mother who swears her house is haunted. She keeps hearing moaning voices and loud bangs coming from her teenage daughter's bedroom," Trisha gave me a knowing look, which I returned with a grin. I'd bet my left shoe that her house wasn't haunted and that her daughter was hiding a boyfriend.

"Fine. Is that it?" I placed my hands on my desk intending to sit down.

"Nope, two more," she held one out to me with a frown, "Doctor what's-his-name keeps calling. Wanting to do more tests."

"Tell him I'm not interested."

"I've done that at least a dozen times. He's not getting the picture. He swears your blood could help save so many lives if you would just give him a few vials."

I pursed my lips. Doctor Ryan was persistent, I'd give him that. But there was no way I was giving him anything. The last thing I needed was some big-headed doctor with dreams of grandeur trying to use my blood as a miracle cure.

"Next time he calls, let me know and I'll deal with him. What's the last one?"

This time Trisha didn't answer immediately. Her brows furrowed and she seemed hesitant to tell me.

"Trisha. Who else called?"

"Forget it," she crumbled up the paper and gave me a tight smile, "Just a bill collector."

"Did I mention that as well as being an angel, I can also tell when you are lying?" I stared her down until she finally threw her hands up in the air.

"Fine. Sid called a few times but I didn't want to tell you because I know how touchy you are about the man—"

"I'm not touchy," I snapped.

"That, right there," she pointed at me, "That's what I'm talking about. The moment anyone mentions him you get pissed."

"No, I don't."

"Yes, you do. Admit it, Mare. You are hurt that your man lied to you," Trisha tapped her blood red nails on the wooden desk, "It's okay to feel, Mary. It's what makes us —"

"Human," I finished for her, "You forget I'm *not* human. I'm not supposed to feel anything but righteous justice for killing

15

demons, and if I ever lay eyes on Sidney again it will be the last time."

"Fine," Trisha gave an exaggerated sigh and then straightened, "So, what happened with Miss Sunshine?"

I sighed and plopped back down in my chair. "I told her I wouldn't help her, is all."

"Geez, Mare," Trisha rolled her eyes, "No wonder Miss Honey-child was so pissed when she left. Slammed the door and everything," she tapped her chin in thought, "you know for a nice girl she sure does curse like a sailor. There were even words in there *I* didn't know."

"Yea, not everyone is who they pretend to be. *I* should know." Even the nicest person in the world might have a soul so dark that the devil himself would be frightened. Gracie Lou was well on her way to being one of them.

"Mary," Trisha stood from the desk and walked over to the chair in front of me, "You can't keep telling people no. We need their money. Those bills aren't going to pay themselves."

"I haven't told everyone no," I argued back as I turned to my computer and then fiddled with the mouse to wake it up.

"First, there was the Dublins."

"Who wanted me to have a séance to speak to their dead son. I'm an angel, not a psychic."

"Then, there was that yummy hunk of man-candy, Thomas," Trisha's eyes went dreamy. While Thomas had been attractive, I'd found myself comparing him to another equally attractive male.

Shaking my head at the thought, I pointed a finger at her, "Who wanted me to stalk his ex-girlfriend."

Trisha frowned at me before throwing her legs over the side of the chair's arms. "And now . . . Gracie Lou. You've got to accept someone, Mary. Unless . . ."

"Unless what?"

The excited smile that spread across her face made me nervous, "You could start telling people you're an angel."

"No," I said firmly, getting to my feet.

"Oh come on, Mare," Trisha whined from her seat, "You'd be an instant celebrity. Then you wouldn't have to worry about money. They'd do talk shows and photo shoots and maybe even a movie!"

"No," I repeated as I grabbed my camera bag and checked that I had all my gear together. One of the only jobs I had said yes to was my normal gig—taking pictures of cheating spouses. I would be popping by said client's sweetie on my way to another job.

"Why not? Don't you want to be famous? Oh!" she jumped up from her seat her back skirt flouncing around her, "I wonder who would play me? It'd definitely have to be someone good. I don't want them to totally Hollywood me and get someone too perky," she crinkled her nose.

I didn't point out that she was just as perky as anyone who would play her. Trisha might dress the part of a goth, but she was as girly as any other eighteen-year-old girl her age. Except, instead of pink and rainbows, she preferred black and fishnets.

"Trisha," I turned to give her a serious look, "I can't go around telling people who I am. Humans can be . . ." I trailed off trying to think of the right word, ". . . finicky."

"Finicky?" she cocked her head to the side, ignoring her black hair—with purple extensions— as it covered half her face.

"While *you* may be all for the existence of celestial beings and demons," I stepped toward her placing a hand on her shoulder, "Not all humans will feel that way. Some will see me as a threat. Or worse . . . something to study. I don't want to spend the rest of my time on earth in some lab. I'm trying to get home, not become famous."

"Oh," she pouted, but then glanced up at me her expression saddened, "What am I going to do when you go back to heaven?"

"I'm sure you'll figure it out," I smiled and chucked her under the chin, "You're a tough girl. I have no doubt you'll land on your feet. And besides," I grabbed my jacket off the back of my chair and slid it on over my shoulder holster, "I can't go back to heaven until I've found my wings and who knows how long *that* will take?"

"Do you want me to do some research? I know we haven't found Ramiel yet but that doesn't mean there aren't some whisperings going on online about your wings," she shrugged a shoulder, "I mean someone has to be bragging about them. Even if they are demons."

"That's a great idea," I patted her on the shoulder on my way to the door, "You hold down the fort, I've got money to make."

"You got it boss angel," she gave me a thumbs-up while striking a silly pose. I shook my head and smiled. Boss angel. The things she comes up with.

2

THUD. FOR THE LAST hour, there has been a constant pounding on the ground. It came from the reception area.

I rolled my eyes and dropped my legs from my desk. I swear Trisha needed a hobby. Or something other than being here all the time.

"What are you doing?" I asked as I rounded the corner.

Trisha stood beside her desk with a black book held high above her head. She must not have heard me come in because she startled, dropping the book suddenly and it made that thud noise as it hit the ground.

"I'm trying to see if God really does know when you disrespect his stuff. Did you feel that?" she asked as she picked the bible up and dropped it again.

I half wanted to tell her yes just so she'd stop bugging me but for all I knew she'd have continued on for the rest of the day. So instead, I snatched the book from the ground and tucked it under my arm. "No, I didn't feel it. I heard it. And you shouldn't drop books whether it be a holy object or not."

"Ah, come on," she whined, clasping her fishnet-gloved hands together in a pleading clasp. "You won't answer my questions, the least you can do is let me experiment."

Aggravated, but not really wanting to listen to her carry on, I tossed the Bible back to her. "Fine. Carry on. But I'm telling you, it doesn't bother me."

She turned the Bible over in her hand with a frown, "What about if I burned it? Would that make a difference?"

Crossing my arms, I leveled my gaze at her. "No, and if you start a fire in my office you will need to worry more about finding another job than if your experiments work."

Put out by my threat she stopped contemplating the Bible and turned back to the desk. When she twisted back around she held had a piece of paper out to me.

"What's this?" I took the paper from her, squinting at the scribbles on it.

"Your next job," Trisha's voice was a bit more gleeful than it should have been.

The paper only had a name, an address, and a time on it. "What do they want?"

Trisha clasped her hands behind her back and rocked back and forth on the heels of her black knee-high boots, "The Jeffersons want you to sit in on their nanny interviews."

While I was all for making money, the tedious jobs that Trisha had signed me up for lately were getting annoying. Last week it was finding someone's lost dog, this week it seemed to be background checks on nannies.

I know I'd said I wasn't a blood hound but it seemed like ever since my assistant found out I was an angel she'd been trying everything she could to put my skills to the test. This was only one of the instances in which she tested me.

"Fine, what time do they need me?"

"Yesterday."

"Seriously?" I cocked a brow at her, "Then they should have asked for me yesterday."

"I'm kidding," she held her hands up in defense, "But seriously, they want you to come by in an hour. They have their final choice picked and need you to make sure everything is good to go and they aren't hiring some pedophile."

I sighed and rubbed a hand over my face. Guess I'll be eating fast food again. I might have a high metabolism, but if I kept eating so many fatty foods I'd have to start worrying about my weight. No one wants a fat angel. Just thinking about it made me shudder.

"Well, you're driving," I pointed at her.

"Don't I always?" she picked up the keys from the table and headed for the door, "You know, eventually I'm going to start charging you a fare for taking you to these jobs. Or you're going to have to learn to drive."

"Well, until that time comes, get a move on. The Jeffersons are waiting," I pushed her slightly from behind. Might as well get this crap over with so I could get back to what I really wanted to do.

Search for Ramiel.

3

THE JEFFERSON'S HOUSE WAS on one of those loops that only had four other houses on it. Each one was identical except for the numbers on the house and a slight variation in exterior color.

"Might as well live in a box," I muttered to myself as we came to a stop.

"What?" Trisha asked, putting the car in park.

"Nothing." I shook my head and got out of the car. When Trisha didn't follow, I stopped, "Aren't you coming?"

She glanced up at the house and then back at me, shaking her head, "Nope. These aren't my kind of people. No need to make them think you are some crazy person. I'll just wait here." she pulled her phone out of her pocket and started to tap away on it.

Frowning at her, I closed the door. Humans cared too much about looks. What they wore, what color their hair was, or how big their nose was. All things that shouldn't decide what kind of person they were on the inside. Like I'd told Trisha before, just because someone looked like a nice person didn't mean they were one. There were plenty of serial killers who seemed like normal ordinary people which had made it so easy for them to get away with their crimes.

I wasn't fooled though. It was hard to get much by me. My lips turned down. Except if they were a half demon. It still peeved me to no end that I hadn't known what Sid was until his father Asmodeus, the demon of lust, said it right to my face. I'd have to be more careful. I couldn't have things like that happen again.

Nodding to myself, I rang the doorbell and waited. There was some shuffling and voices before the door opened to reveal a cookie-cutter couple.

Both in pale cream shirts, they were dark-haired and dark-eyed, the only difference between them was the fake smile on the wife's face and the purely sexual one on the husband's.

Ignoring the way he was looking at me, I offered my hand to the wife, "Hello, I'm Mary. You called for my help picking your nanny?"

"Hello!" Mrs. Jefferson said with an over-enthusiastic tone. Her eyes swept up and down my form, reflecting clear disapproval. "You'll have to excuse us, you weren't what we were expecting."

I didn't respond. I wasn't exactly sure what she had expected. Someone in a multi-colored skirt and a head wrap? If they wanted that, I could have gotten Madame Serena, the psychic who ran the shop below my office, to come in my stead. Of course, Madame Serena's gifts were a bit touch-and-go there was no telling what she would tell them.

I, on the other hand, wasn't going to change my usual outfit of jeans and a t-shirt to try to impress a couple of humans who probably wouldn't even remember me after I left.

After a few awkward moments, Mrs. Jefferson nudged her husband in the side, her fake smile cracking on her face. The husband finally stopped staring at my chest long enough to say, "Well, no matter. We are happy to have you. Come right this way."

They moved aside to let me into their home. We walked down an off-white hallway and into the living room. The ceilings were high and the space open enough to see the kitchen from the couch. I stopped in the middle of the room where a little girl not much more than three with a head full of dark curls sat on the ground playing with blocks.

"This is our precious girl, Brittany. She'll be four this year," Mrs. Jefferson told me though I hadn't asked. I'd noticed humans tended to do that. Offering up information to anyone who would listen. A bad trait in my business. Demons wouldn't hesitate to use any information you gave them against you.

I knelt on the floor next to Brittany who glanced up from her blocks and smiled at me.

"Hello," I smiled back at her. Before I could say another word the toddler was discarding her blocks and climbing into my lap.

"Oh, Brittany," her mother tried to stop her but I waved her off.

"How are you?" I asked her. I didn't use a high-pitched voice like most humans did when talking to a child. Instead, I addressed her the way I would an adult.

"Are you an angel?" she asked completely bypassing my question.

My eyes crinkled and my smile widened. "Not at the moment. I seemed to have misplaced my wings. But when I get them back I will be."

Brittany giggled, "You're funny."

"Now that's enough Brittany. Mary has some work to do," Mr. Jefferson said causing the child to frown and climb off of my lap.

I stood to my feet and turned away from the toddler who started to play with her blocks once more. "It's no bother really. Children have always been drawn to me."

"I suppose it has something to do with your gifts," Mrs. Jefferson offered me a smile though it didn't reach her eyes. I had a feeling that she was not the one who had wanted me to come.

"They do come in handy," I offered up and then glanced around, "So where is this nanny you wanted me to check out?"

"Oh, she should be here any moment. We wanted to meet you first before she got here," Mrs. Jefferson said and then gestured for me to have a seat on one of their beige couches.

Sitting down, I crossed one leg over the other a move that did not go unnoticed by the husband. Placing my hands in my lap, I waited for them to decide on a point of conversation. I was happy to just sit there until the nanny arrived, but most humans didn't like silence. At one point, I hadn't either.

The scars on my back twanged in memory.

A portal had been opened between the earth realm and hell. Ramiel had gone to check that no demons had gotten through but when he hadn't returned, everyone had assumed he was a goner. But not me.

Reckless and over confident, I had charged down to earth intent on saving my commander. What I hadn't expected was the few dozen demons waiting at the portal. And that was when they'd taken me.

They had thrown me into a dark room with no windows and a hard floor. When they'd shut the door behind me there had only been silence. It could have minutes, or weeks, before they finally remembered I was down there. By that time, I had already begun to go crazy from being cut off from God's holy presence, and the silence had just made it worse. I was little more than a rampaging animal with only one purpose. Escape.

"Mary?"

"I'm sorry . . . what?" I shook my head, clearing my thoughts and glanced to Mrs. Jefferson.

She pursed her lips, "I said the nanny is here. Do you want to start?" she gestured to a young woman—who looked to be in her early twenties—standing next to Mr. Jefferson.

"Oh, sorry. Sure, we can start now," I nodded to the girl.

"So . . ." Mr. Jefferson trailed off, "Do you need us to leave the room or . . .?"

"Nope," I answered and stood from my seat. I walked over to the young woman and looked her over. Her dark hair was pulled up in a high ponytail that brushed her back. She wore shorts that went to mid-thigh and a t-shirt that claimed she went to Los Angeles City College. Overall, she looked like the typical college student, not a pedophile. Why they'd thought that would be a problem was beyond me.

The nanny who no one had bothered to introduce to me, shuffled from foot to foot, her eyes darting to Mr. Jefferson and his wife every so often. Nervous but not more than the usual when applying for a new job.

Nodding to myself, I was about to do the final check by dropping the veil that kept me from seeing inside of everyone all the time when Mrs. Jefferson spoke up.

"Are you going to do something, or what? We aren't paying you to stand there."

I sighed. I hated this part about my job. Everyone expected light shows and smoke but most powers are not so flashy. Sure, if there was a demon to be dispossessed then there might be some smoke, but a regular soul reading really wasn't that interesting.

"I *am* trying to do that job," I explained, trying not to snap at her. Like the woman had said, she *was* paying me. Trisha would bite my head off if I didn't get paid again because of my attitude. It happened more often than I liked, that was, when I actually remembered to ask them for money.

"But don't you need to wave some incense or something? Say a chant?" Mrs. Jefferson waved a hand at me.

"Not unless you really want me to," I crinkled my nose. Incense always made me sneeze, "Look, you hired me to check out your nanny. That's what I'm doing. Now, I can't do my job if you keep asking me questions."

Mrs. Jefferson narrowed her eyes at me but didn't say anything else.

Letting out a relieved breath, I turned back to the young woman who had become even more nervous by our exchange. I gave her a small smile, "Just relax. It won't hurt. You won't even know I'm doing anything."

The nanny's shoulders relaxed and she gave a short nod, "Okay."

Without warning, I dropped the veil and peered at the nanny. I searched her over and when I didn't find anything too bad, I turned my attention to my employers.

Mrs. Jefferson's soul was cleaner than I would have thought for her snooty attitude. It was so white it was almost saintly. Her husband on the other hand . . .

Mr. Jefferson's wasn't black, but it was muddier than I would have liked for a father. He might not be a pedophile, but he sure as heck wasn't a nice person.

I closed my eyes, forcing the veil to come back up in place. When I opened my eyes the husband was staring at me. Hard. Returning his stare with one of my own, I smirked as he broke the connection first.

"Well?"

I turned to Mrs. Jefferson and said, "Your nanny is clean. Though I maybe wouldn't keep money or jewelry laying out." My words caused the nanny to stiffen next to me.

"Thank you very much for your time Mary," Mr. Jefferson tried to usher me out of the house, but I shook him off.

"And as for your husband . . ."

"That's enough," Mr. Jefferson snapped, "We hired you to read the nanny, not us. You'll get your check in the mail."

"Now, wait a minute," Mrs. Jefferson stepped in with a frown, "I want to know what she saw. That is unless you have something you would like to tell me, Bill?"

Bill Jefferson crossed his arms over his chest and frowned, "Of course I don't, Joan. I can assure you anything else this fraud has to say isn't worth listening to."

"Hey," I glared at Bill, "Not wanting to hear what I have to say is one thing but I won't let you blatantly lie to save your own skin," I then turned my attention to Joan, "Your husband is not a nice man. Maybe not a murderer, but I can bet there's something shady going on in his life that he's hiding from you," I scanned him up and down, a sneer on my face, "Definitely something to do with sex, that much is clear."

The guy hadn't been able to keep his eyes off me and when the nanny had come in he had stood unusually close to her. Pornography would have been one thing, but it wouldn't have made his soul so muddy. I was betting it was prostitutes, or even worse, sex slaves.

Joan gasped behind me and I didn't wait to hear what she had to say before I moved out of their line of fire and out of the house. There was no way I was getting paid. Trisha was going to be so pissed.

I got to the car just as my cell phone rang. The caller I.D. said it was the police station. Good. I needed a job to make up for this one.

"Hey, please tell me you have a dead body for me or something," I answered, expecting to hear Sergeant Thompson's voice on the other line.

"Is this Mary Wiles?" an unfamiliar voice asked.

Sobering up, I cleared my throat, "Yes, this is her. Who's this?"

"This is Detective Riley. I have a Sidney Magnus in holding. He claims he knows you and since I know you work with the Sergeant sometimes, I thought I'd give you a call to follow up his story. So, do you?"

"Do I what?"

"Know Sidney Magnus?"

"And if I say no?"

"Then he'll be held here until his hearing where he will be prosecuted to the full extent of the law," the detective said, a bit more smug than I had expected.

I chewed on my lip for a moment, contemplating hanging up. If Sidney had gotten himself into trouble it was probably something demon-related. Which meant that I needed to know what he was up to.

With a reluctant sigh, I answered, "I know him. Tell Thompson I'm on my way."

Hanging up the phone, I jumped into the car where Trisha turned to me. "So where to next boss angel?"

4

TRISHA HAD TO GET home so I took a taxi to the LAPD precinct. Why Sid had called me to bail him out is beyond me. We weren't exactly on the best of terms since we last saw each other.

Sid had been one of my closest friends once upon a time. That was before I'd found out he had been hiding a big secret from me. Not a my-middle-name-is-Pubert kind of secret but a I'm-really-a-half-demon-whose-father-just-tried-to-kill-your-best-friend kind of secret.

Safe to say, I didn't particularly like him right now. What was even worse was he had stolen my first human experience by using his demon mojo on me. Had it not been for him, I'd have happily gone on through the human world without ever wondering about the tingling feeling I got around certain males.

They're right when they said ignorance is bliss. And right now, I needed a whole heaping amount of ignorance. I wanted to un-know what it felt like to have his lips pressed against mine. To know how it felt to have the burn of desire run through my veins.

Sid had a lot to make up for.

Shaking my head, I took a deep breath before walking into the police station. As usual, the station was buzzing with activity. Officers coming in and out, suspects being carted to an interview room or a cell. There was always a line of criminals sitting off to the side. If it hadn't been a police station, you'd think they were just waiting to go to an appointment, but many of them were just waiting to get be processed.

There weren't enough officers to handle all the bad happening in Los Angeles. It would be even worse if a real demon got through to this plane. Not those body jumpers, but a real life demon lord. You wouldn't need to be supernatural to know they were coming. Their power was so tangible that even the most closed-off human would know something was up. A tingle down their spine. A sick feeling in their stomach. Some kind of reaction from their soul warning them away, though most humans failed to listen to those feelings and that's what got them killed.

"Wiles!"

My eyes turned from scanning the room to Sergeant Thompson waving his hand at me. I held a hand up to let him know I'd seen him and in response he gestured for me to come into his office.

Heading through the maze of desks, I nodded and said hello to some of the various officers. When I wasn't catching cheating spouses or exorcising demons, I sometimes helped the LAPD out with their occult cases. For the police force one would think they would have it covered, but after a few years of working with them, I had learned they knew diddly squat about demons and supernatural entities. Just by chance I'd met Thompson and started working with him.

41

Though, I wouldn't say it had benefited me much. My large hospital bill could attest to that.

"Hey, Thompson," I sat down in the chair across from his desk crossing my hands over my stomach. My Glock 42 pressed against my side, its position revealing the butt of the gun to the Sergeant.

"You know, you really shouldn't wear that when you aren't working," Thompson's gray eyes stared at my gun from beneath bushy eyebrows. Built like a linebacker, the Sergeant could scare any officer into cooperating with just a single look, but I just brushed it off. There were scarier things in this world than an overly large man.

"After the last time?" I raised a brow at him. "I don't think so. I am armed all the time, and loaded with holy bullets."

Thompson frowned, "Isn't that a bit of overkill?"

"Not when a demon lord is on the loose," I leaned back in my chair and placed my feet on the desk in front of me.

"But I thought you killed him back at the warehouse," Thompson glared at my feet but didn't push them off. Smart man.

"I killed his host, yeah, but if you think a measly holy bullet is enough to kill a demon lord for good, then you're in for a rude awakening."

When Trisha had been captured by the demon of lust, Asmodeus—also known as Sid's dad—I'd had to rescue her with Sid's own gun. The fact that I had shot him with his son's gun had some poetry to it. And I was stupid enough to think that he was gone for good. The body might be dead but there was nothing stopping him from grabbing another one and trying to cross over to the human world again. And since I was the one who'd ruined his last attempt, I had no doubt he would come after me given the chance.

"So then why don't you just hunt the guy down and blast him back to hell, or whatever?" he gestured a beefy finger to the ground as if Hell was beneath us. I didn't bother to correct him. Hell wasn't somewhere you could physically dig through the earth and get to. Why would God make it that easy for the demons to attack his precious creations? If could just accidentally stumble across it, the whole human world would be overrun by hell-beasts by now.

"It's not that easy," I shook my head, "And not something that I can explain in a few minutes' time. Besides," I stood from my seat. "I'm here for something else."

Thompson stared at me for a moment as if trying to decide if he was going to drop the subject. Finally, after a few seconds, he pushed himself to his feet as well.

"You're here for the bartender guy, Sid," he stated, opening the door of his office for me. The hustle and bustle of the precinct filled my senses.

"So what did he do?" I asked as I followed Thompson between the maze of desks and over to the holding cells.

"He's your boyfriend. Shouldn't you know?" he gave me a teasing grin and I flipped him off. His face sobered and he stopped before the entrance to the cells, "Look, I don't know what kind of stuff your guy is into, but he helped us out last month and cops don't forget those kinds of things. But if he is going to go breaking

44

and entering, tell him to lay off the VIPs okay?"

"Breaking and entering?" I asked as Thompson got the clerk to let him through the first door.

"Yeah," he said over his shoulder, "your guy might be great with demons but he sucks when it comes to stealing. He hadn't gotten one foot in the door of the place before the alarms went off."

I followed behind him as he led me down a row of cells. He stopped at the last one and then turned to me. "He picked the wrong house to break into, that's for sure. Even though he hadn't gotten away with anything the owner's want to him to see jail-time. But since this is a first offense and there is no proof he'd actually been there to steal anything, the judge let him off with a hefty fine."

Thompson banged on the bars of the cell causing the three occupants to look up. One was a teenager who seemed ready to wet himself at any moment, another one a large muscled man with tattoos and a mean grin. The last one had a dark head of hair, and piercing green eyes that even now made me weak in the knees.

45

Get a hold of yourself, Mary.

"Magnus, you're up." Thompson hollered at him causing Sid to get to his feet.

He tucked his hands in the pockets of his tight jeans his dark blue t-shirt clinging to his chest as he approached the bars. "Angel, I didn't think you'd come."

Even the sound of his voice made my body react. I might be mad at him mentally, but my body didn't agree. Though, I could probably chalk that up to his demon powers. Son of the demon of lust and all.

"Well, if you are doing something illegal it is probably demon related. I couldn't very well leave you here without finding out what it is," I responded matter of factly.

Sid frowned, "That's all?" Thompson opened the door to the cell and I stepped back as Sid came out and moved in on me. "You only want to know what I'm up to? You didn't come to see me?"

"If I wanted to see you I would have answered the dozens of messages you've left me," I snarled.

"Okay, you lovebirds. You can fight later," Thompson stepped between us. "We have to get you signed out and then you can rip each other's throats out. Or make out, or whatever it is you kids do these days."

Thompson led us out of the holding area and into the reception area. He handed Sid some papers to sign and then I had to sign something saying that I was taking him into my custody. Though, what I was supposed to do with him after we left the precinct was a mystery to me.

After all the papers were signed and Thompson left us, we were utterly alone.

I stood in the reception area with my arms over my chest, not sure what to say. After a moment, Sid ran his hand through his hair and stepped toward me. I took a half step back, which caused him to stop and sigh.

"I'm not going to hurt you, angel."

"Stop calling me that," I snapped, "I'm not your friend. You're," I lowered my voice, "a demon. You're lucky I don't shoot you right here."

"But if you do that then you won't find out that I was breaking into and entering the most renowned artifact collector in the city. They've got some pretty rare stuff." he smirked at me before heading out the precinct doors.

Grumbling under my breath, I followed after him. I came up next to him at the top of the steps to the police station and asked, "Fine, I won't shoot you until *after* you tell me."

"Man, you really don't know how to lie do you?" he quirked a brow at me.

"I don't see the point," I shrugged, "and besides, why should I lie to you? You've lied enough for the both of us."

"If you are going to keep insulting me, I'll just find my own way home," Sid started down the stairs waving at me over his shoulder.

"Where's your truck?" I glanced around the lot and my eyes landed on his large 4x4 black truck, "Why don't you just take it?"

Sid stopped and glanced back at me, "Suspended license."

"What'd you do now?" I rolled my eyes not even sure I wanted to know.

"Nothing," Sid shrugged, "Your friend Thompson might have pulled some strings

48

for me, but apparently breaking and entering still has consequences. They think I'll be less likely to get in any more trouble if I can't drive for a while," he scoffed and rubbed his chin, "Like the thousands of dollars I have to pay isn't bad enough."

"Well, I don't know what to tell you. I was going to take a taxi?" I pulled my phone out of my pocket bringing up the number to the taxi agency I usually used.

"Where's Trisha?" Sid glanced around, "Isn't she usually your chauffeur?"

"Sent her home. I didn't know how long this would take and I didn't want to keep her too late in case her parents got upset," I put the phone to my ear and waited for the operator to pick up.

"Happy Taxi, how can we help you?" an overly-perky voice answered the phone.

"Hi, I need a pickup," I rambled off the address to the West L.A. precinct.

"And when do you need a pickup by?"

Before I could answer, the phone was pulled from my hands. "Hey!" I turned to glare at Sid who had my phone up to his ear.

"Never mind. We have a ride," he hung up the phone and tossed it to me. I quickly caught it before it hit the ground. I had already lost one phone in the last month. I wasn't about to lose another one.

"What'd you do that for?" I clenched my teeth. Had he always been this annoying?

"Come on, you don't need to waste your money on something like that. I have a vehicle," he started into the parking lot once more.

"Yeah, that you can't drive," I pointed out as I hustled after him.

"You have a license don't you?" he turned around so he was walking backward.

Technically, yes, I did have a license. It was fake, as was the rest of my documentation. My friend Adara had helped me out so I could pass for human. I'd learned quickly that people would screw you over easily if you didn't have the right documentation.

"I don't know how to drive," I glanced at his truck with a frown.

"That's okay. It's easy. I'll show you," he tossed me his keys and went to the passenger side of the car.

When I didn't immediately climb into the driver's seat he poked his head out of the door and yelled, "Are you coming or what?"

My lips twisted into a grimace as I stared down at the keys in my hands. If I did this I wouldn't be able to use the I-can't-drive excuse with Trisha anymore. But the thought of learning to drive kind of excited me. I'd heard it was one of the closest things to flying for humans.

And God did I miss that feeling.

Lips curled up in a grin, I jumped into the truck. Once I was in the seat I froze. What did I do now?

"You really haven't ever been behind a wheel before, have you?" Sid chuckled making my grin fall.

"No."

Leaning toward me so that I could smell the spicy scent of him, he took the keys from my hands and stuck it in a hole next to the steering wheel. He turned the key making the truck purr to life.

"Now, lucky for you this is an automatic, so you just have to steer and get your feet right," Sid pointed a finger at where my feet were. "There are two pedals down there, the one on the right is the gas and the one on the left is the brake."

"So, I just push this," I pushed my foot down on the gas making the sound coming from the truck become louder. But we didn't move.

"Yes, but you have to move out of park first," he gestured to a stick next to the steering wheel, "Push the brake and move this until the D symbol lights up."

I did as he said and then as soon as the little D lit up, I switched my foot over to the gas. The truck shot forward like a rocket and I quickly shoved both feet onto the brake.

"Jesus, Mary. Not so hard," Sid cried out clutching his side of the car like his life depended on it.

Smirking at his reaction, I slowly pressed the gas once more. This was going to be fun.

5

SID GIVING ME THE keys to his truck was an idiot move on his part. But with some stop-and-go, and a whole lot of yelling from the passenger seat, I finally got us on the road.

He directed me to St. Michael's Cathedral, a destination that had me raising an eyebrow at him. But I didn't say anything.

When we arrived, I put the truck into park and glanced up at the church. It was like all the others. Overly-large with stained glass windows and wooden double doors. More overbearing than welcoming to me.

"Why did you want to come here?" I asked as Sid opened the door. "Aren't you afraid God will smite you for crossing his threshold?" I gave a bitter lopsided grin.

"You know for an angel you sure are judgmental," Sid said before slamming the door shut behind him.

I quickly unbuckled and scrambled out of the truck behind him. "Now wait a minute. I'm not judgmental."

"Could have fooled me," he scoffed, taking the church stairs two at a time.

Fists clenched I caught up to him before he could open the church door. "Hey buddy, I'm not the one who was lying for years about what I was. That was you."

"Pot calling kettle." he pointed at me to him.

"What's that supposed to mean?" I frowned and crossed my arms over my chest.

"Tell me this," he leaned forward into my space until I could smell that addicting scent of his, and I forced myself not to lean back. "When exactly were you going to tell Trisha you were an angel?"

My mouth dropped open and then I frowned hard. "That's different."

"Exactly," he smirked, jerking the church door open.

I stared at him for a moment before following him inside.

The interior was no more impressive than every other church I had been to. Marble statues, rows of pews, and even a large wooden cross sat at the top of the stage area.

Sid kept walking until he stopped at the line of candles that the Priest left out for those who wished to pray for loved ones. I came up beside him as he lit one of the wicks.

"Does God hear the prayers of demons?" I inquired.

"Who knows?" Sid shrugged one masculine shoulder his dark eyes on me. "You are the better one to answer that than me, angel."

The sound of my nickname on his lips made my throat close up. I swallowed thickly and gazed up at the cross before us so I wouldn't have to look at him.

"You know I would have told her eventually," I continued from earlier just to fill the silence. "I just hadn't found the right moment yet."

"And that's different from me and you how?"

"It's entirely different. For one," I pointed a finger at him. "Neither of us is human and we both know humans are unpredictable when faced with the unknown and I try to keep Trisha as much out of the supernatural bit of the business as possible."

Sid chuckled. "That's a thin excuse. Trisha is smarter than most humans her age and older. And keeping it from her didn't do you much good of keeping her out of it now did it?"

He had a point there. Though, Trisha knowing I wasn't human wouldn't have helped her from getting kidnapped or almost being sacrificed to Sid's dad a month ago. All it's done so far is cause me a headache with all her pestering.

"Well, if you hadn't been keeping your secret from me, you could have warned me about your dad and then maybe Trisha wouldn't have been taken," I argued back smugly.

"Fine," Sid snapped getting to his feet, "You want me to admit I was wrong?" he didn't wait for me to answer, "I was wrong. I'm sorry I should have told you. Are you happy now?"

No. Not really. I wanted him to take away the feelings he caused in me. The longing that I have felt ever since we kissed. But I didn't say any of that. Instead I said, "So why did you want to come here anyways?"

Sid's brows narrowed at my change of subject and then he heaved a big sigh, thankfully not pushing the subject. "I come here to pray for my mother and . . ." he unwound the rosary around his wrist, "This was given to me by the Priest that used to run this parish. It has to be blessed every few weeks or it loses its abilities."

"Abilities?"

He gave me a dark look, "You didn't think I passed as a human on my own, do you?"

I shrugged. How the hell should I know? I might know more about demons than most humans but I don't know much about half-demons. If anything.

"While I might be half demon, I am also half human. Meaning both sides of me are constantly fighting for control. This . . ." he held the rosary up to my gaze, "helps me to control my demon side."

I leaned forward inspecting the rosary closely. It didn't look any different than any other rosary, but then again my talisman didn't look like much to the average person. I counted on that to get the jump on demons.

"So what happens if you don't get it blessed?"

"The demon part of me leaks out," he wrapped the beads back around his wrist, "Ever notice how sometimes I get moodier than normal? Or when the tension in the bar is so thick you feel like you are walking through soup?"

I nodded. I knew what he was talking about. On more than one occasion he had acted out of his normal flirty character and had practically bitten my head off. But I'd always chalked it up to him just being grumpy, not his demonic side taking over. Though, come to think of it, the couple I'd witnessed practically having intercourse on the bar's dance floor did come to mind.

My eyes widened and then I glared, "You used your powers on me, didn't you?"

"What?"

"It all makes sense now," I continued as if he hadn't spoken, "That's why you affect me so, and why I let you kiss me. You," I pointed an accusing finger at him, "used your demon-of-lust powers against me."

Sid's eyes crinkled at the corners and his lips ticked up before he suddenly began to laugh. Anger ate at me for being so foolish to fall for his tricks, and his laughter didn't help any.

"Let me get this straight," Sid said in between heavy breaths, "You think I used some demon magic to make you want me?"

I frowned at the tone of his voice, "Of course. It's the only logical explanation."

"And it never crossed your angelic mind that I might just be that sexy?"

Now he was just screwing with me, "More like full of it," hands on my hips, I leaned toward him and growled, "Over five years on earth and not once have I had any interest in having physical contact with anyone human or otherwise but you show up and suddenly I can't control my body temperature and I find myself admiring your muscles in more than a soldier's appreciation way," I gestured toward his thick arms which flexed under my gaze.

Sid chuckled once more, "That, angel, is called attraction and here's a news flash for you," he took a step toward me until I could feel his body heat on my skin, "While my father might be the demon of lust, I couldn't make a dog like me, let alone an angel. I can intensify emotions that are already there but that's all."

I locked my lips his closeness making my brain get that mushy feeling again and I had to shake my head to get rid of it. I stepped away from him and scowled, "Bullshit. I couldn't possibly be attracted to the likes of you."

"Oh, but you are," he grinned, a bit of smugness in his tone.

I crossed my arms tightly over my chest, my hand gripping the butt of my gun underneath my arm until it bit into my hand. It wasn't true. He was lying. Demons don't tell the truth, even when it would benefit them.

"Just admit it, angel. You'll feel better for it."

"Never," I growled.

His brow scrunched together at my reaction. "What bothers you more? That you are becoming more human? Or that it's a demon that you are attracted to?"

Which one? Both. Neither. I didn't really know.

On the one hand, if I was only attracted to him because I was becoming more human then that meant I had less time to find Ramiel and get my wings back than I'd thought. On the other hand, being attracted to a demon was not high on my to-do list. It was more on my never-in-a-million-years list and even then the likelihood was slim to none.

"You'll never find out because I'm not attracted to you," I shoved past him and started down the aisle toward the exit.

"I could help you find what you are looking for, you know," his voice echoed after me, making me pause.

I turned back to glare at him, "What do you know about it?"

He tucked his hands into his jean pockets and languidly moved toward me, "I know you are looking for your wings."

"That's not really a secret. Even the lesser demons know I'm looking for them. I'm sure it's just a big laugh to you guys down there. Probably have them mounted somewhere so you can all stand around and talk about how they bested Muriel."

"I wouldn't know," Sid shrugged, "I've never been there. Half human, remember? But I do know a thing or two about the whereabouts of a certain archangel."

The taunting in his voice just daring me to ask him made my blood boil. He'd admitted it to make me ask him where Ramiel was. Besides the flowers he'd sent while I was in the hospital, I hadn't seen or heard from my former commander. But that didn't mean I was so desperate I'd ask a demon. Not after what they did to me. Besides, I still had an ace up my sleeve. That is if Adara ever got back to me.

"No, thanks," I spun around. I completely expected him to call after me. I hadn't walked more than a few steps away before Sid was behind me.

"Come on, angel. Don't be like that. I just want to make it up to you." When I didn't stop, or acknowledge him, he grabbed my arm.

"Let go of me."

"Never," he pulled on my arm until I had no choice but to step into his embrace to avoid falling over. It just so happened that

I was faster. The moment he had his arms around me, I had my gun out and pointed at Sid's chest.

"Don't ever touch me again. You might be part human but the other part is still a demon, and I won't hesitate to take you out."

He glanced down at my gun, not as worried as I would have liked about its position, "Didn't we do this once before? We both know you won't do it."

I dropped the gun and jerked away from him. "No, but keep pushing me and that little bit stopping me won't matter anymore. Then you'll just be as dead as the rest of them."

6

AFTER DROPPING SID OFF, I called a taxi to get home. It was well after dark and I wasn't about to call Trisha to come pick me up. Knowing her she'd give me the third degree about what happened between Sid and me.

I so didn't want to deal with her probing questions.

Getting out of the taxi, I glanced up at my building. Its two stories wasn't that nice to look at, but the crime rate was pretty low and there was a really good Chinese place that had set up shop next door. Thinking about the Chinese reminded me that I hadn't gotten Trisha to stop on the way to the precinct, and now I was starving.

Set on ordering some take-out, I was stopped only by the sound of Madame Serena calling my name.

"Hey Serena," I greeted her with a wave. Madame Serena owned the shop below my office and was also my landlord. I'd never had any trouble from her except when she tried to read my fortune. She was always wrong.

"Late night?" her eyes scanned me as if looking for some invisible sign that would tell her what I had been up to.

"Not too late, thankfully," I gave her a small smile. It was only a bit after nine and if I could get out of this conversation fast enough I could still get some Chow Mein.

"I saw a dark man in your future Mary," Madame Serena waved her hand across the air between us causing her bangles to clink together. "Perhaps an old lover? Or a new one?" she gave me a knowing grin.

I shook my head and laughed, "Nope no lovers for me. I've got too much on my plate to worry about men," Especially, when those men were dark-haired. I only knew one dark-haired man and I had just

65

left him at church to pray, or to do whatever it was he was really doing there.

"You shouldn't work so hard," Madame Serena chastised, "A young woman like yourself should be enjoying her life, not working all the time."

"Working pays the bills," *Sometimes*, I thought wearily, remembering my last job at the Jeffersons'. I really needed to learn to keep my mouth shut.

"Well, you be sure to take care of yourself. Working is all good, but not if you're dead. Eight hours of sleep and three meals a day. Don't go skimping on your basic health," she said, looking me up and down as if I were a pile of skin and bones.

Holding my hands up, I chuckled, "Don't worry I will. I was just about to go grab something from Lou's next door."

Madame Serena's lips twisted and her gaze shot to the Chinese place before coming back to me, "You be careful. That Lou is a stinker. Keeps forgetting my fortune cookie!"

"I will be. You have a nice night, Serena," I waved and backed away. Madame Serena always complained about the restaurant owner Lou. If it wasn't fortune cookies today it was too much sauce the next. I'd secretly thought that they had a thing going on, but who was I to say? I hadn't even been able to tell that I was attracted to someone until recently.

Thankfully, I'd missed the dinner rush and had my order in hand in under ten minutes. With my Chinese in hand, I made my way up the stairs to my office slash apartment.

There wasn't a kitchen but I had a mini fridge for any necessary cold items. Since I didn't cook, and didn't plan on learning to anytime soon, I figured why spend the extra money I didn't have on getting a real apartment. I hadn't been lying when I'd said my work was my life.

I ate, slept, and breathed my job. Of course, my day job as a Private Detective helped pay the bills, but my real job was hunting down the demons who had taken my wings and who I suspected had taken Ramiel too. Though, I had no real proof. I hadn't even known Ramiel was still alive until I had received a bouquet of flowers from him while I was in the hospital. Since then I had changed my focus from demons to finding my commanding officer.

Speaking of which, I sat my Chinese down on my desk and pulled my phone out. Tapping Adara's number I waited for her to pick up.

"Hey, girl. What's up?" Adara's voice called out on the other end. It had a bit of an echo to it.

"Am I on speaker phone?" I asked while digging through my bag for my food.

"Yeah," she said, her voice echoing again, "Hold on a sec," she shuffled a few things around and something fell that caused her to curse before she came back on, "Sorry about that. I had my hands full. I can talk now. What's up?"

Opening the container of Chow Mein, I moved the food around with my fork as I asked, "I was checking in to see if you had any leads?"

Adara, an ex-demon hunter, focused more on the vampire type half-breeds than the real thing, but it still gave her many connections I didn't have. I'd asked her to check those connections to see if anyone had heard anything about an angel, fallen or otherwise.

"I'm sorry, Mary, but no one has heard anything," I could hear the dejection in her voice. Not that I didn't trust Adara. She was one of the only people I trusted with all my secrets. I had never had to lie to her about who, or what I was. Not that I could have since *she* was the one who had saved me.

When I'd finally come crawling out of hell, I'd been beaten and bloodied so badly that I'd barely been able to stand let alone fight off an attacker. Lucky for me, the portal I had escaped through had landed me in the woods. I'd dragged myself through the trees, my back aflame and my body almost useless until I hadn't been able to move anymore. I'd collapsed somewhere there in the woods.

Next thing I remembered was waking up in a wooden cottage with Adara sitting next to me. She had cleaned and bandaged my wounds, and sat by my side the whole time I was out. Even when I woke and attacked her, she hadn't left me.

Being tortured by demons for days on end for God only knew how long did something to a person, even an angel. I was little more than an animal when she found me. It took weeks before I could think like myself again. Then months for me to finally have enough strength to talk about what happened.

Adara had listened to my story never once asking a question until the end. I had told her what I was and everything, and the only thing she could ask was, "Do you want revenge?"

Since then she has been the one I ran to if I was in trouble, or at my wit's end. Adara knew what it was like to need to get back at those who had hurt us. She had her own dark past, ending with a dead lover and a disowned father. She'd left her hunter's guild after that and had been freelancing ever since. She didn't really hunt demons anymore, but sometimes I could tell she had the itch to get back in the game. I think she lived vicariously through me sometimes. Just to feel like she was still in the game.

I sighed irritably and stabbed at my Chow Mein. "Well, do you have any other places you could check? I mean, I had Trisha use all her hacking abilities to try and hunt him down based on the flowers he left. But nothing."

There hadn't been anything leading to Ramiel. He'd paid cash for the flowers through a delivery service. He'd placed the order through a prepaid phone that wasn't in use anymore. Even hunting his phone down had been a dead end. It seemed Ramiel was better at keeping under the radar than I was.

"Mary," Adara said in her tone of voice that I knew meant she was about to say something I wasn't going to like, "Maybe Ramiel doesn't want to be found?"

"I don't care," I snapped, taking a large bit of my meal. I chomped down on the noodles with more aggression than needed, "If he didn't want to be found then he shouldn't have let me know he was alive by sending those flowers."

"Are you sure they were even from him?" Adara asked, disbelief in her voice.

"No doubt about it. Only he knew that I liked those kinds of flowers. I'd made a comment about them the one time we had a mission together on earth rounding up some demons. I was supposed to be his healer in case things got nasty," Thinking about my time with my former

71

commanding made a fist tighten around my heart.

"And you are sure he didn't tell anyone? Maybe they tortured it out of him?" I scoffed at her suggestion.

"Believe me, they might torture him for secrets from heaven but definitely not for my favorite flower."

Just the thought of it was ridiculous.

"Then there has to be some other explanation. Could it be his way of telling you he's okay but not to come after him? Maybe he knew you were in trouble and didn't want you to get hurt more by looking for him?"

I shook my head and then remembered she couldn't see me, "No, no way. Why would he do that? He knows me too well to think that letting me know he is alive would be enough for me. He had to have known it would set me off. Now, I just have to figure out why he's hiding from me."

There was silence for a moment and I almost thought Adara had hung up before she started talking again and this time her voice was dangerously low.

"I don't want to be the one to have to bring this up but maybe . . ." she stopped and gave a short laugh, "No, never mind. Forget it. I think I'm getting too bitter in my old age."

Frowning at her abrupt stop, I leaned forward in my seat, my full attention on the phone, "No, what were you going to say? I'm at my wits end here, anything would help."

Adara gave a heavy sigh, "I was just thinking that maybe Ramiel hadn't been captured. That maybe, just maybe, he had left willingly."

I was quiet for a moment. It wasn't unheard of for angels to fall. There was a whole league of them who fell when Lucifer had revolted. But the thought of Ramiel, my commander, my best friend in all of heaven, falling without me knowing? That was unspeakable.

"No," I stated firmly, "Not possible."

"I'm just saying, it could have happened. You never saw him and —"

"No," this time I snapped, "Ramiel isn't like that. He couldn't have. Not without telling me first."

"Alright, alright. Don't bite my head off. I was just trying to look at it from a different perspective," Adara tried to pacify me.

"I know," I sighed and plopped back in my chair, my appetite suddenly gone.

"I just don't want you wasting your time here hunting for someone who doesn't want to be found. Isn't your whole focus on getting your wings so you can get back to heaven?"

"Yes, but now that I know he's alive I just can't ignore it," I rubbed a hand over my face, "Are you sure there is no one else you can ask?"

"I'll ask around some more, but you should think about using your own connections."

Frowning at the phone, I said, "What connections?"

"You know the demon variety. More specifically, a hot half-demon who you have been avoiding. I'm sure if you used your charms you could rustle up some answers or even just a good wrestle would do you some good." The teasing tone in her voice would have made me smile except for the subject of her teasing.

"I actually just saw him and he's even worse than before I knew he was a half-demon," I scowled thinking of my last conversation with Sid, "And I doubt he knows anything. He's too busy running errands for his daddy." A light bulb when off in my head and I cursed.

"What? Did you think of something?" Adara asked. "Did you guys kiss again?"

"No," I growled, "and remind me never to tell you anything ever again."

Adara laughed, "Like that would happen. So what is it then, if not some juicy gossip?"

I shook my head to myself, she would never change, "I just remembered I forgot to make Sid tell me what he was up to."

"What he's up to?"

"Yeah, he got arrested for breaking and entering and I'm sure it has something to do with demons, I stood from my chair and headed over to the couch. I pulled the cushions from the top and yanked the handle that unfolded my bed.

"How do you know he isn't just really into stealing stuff?" Adara asked as I sat down on the bed and began to untie my boots.

"I highly doubt that," I pressed the phone to my face and shoulder as I tossed one boot, and then the other, off.

"So then it's perfect timing."

"How so?" I struggled out of my jeans and then slipped off my shoulder holster, setting it on the nightstand by the bed. I used to keep it in the drawer of my desk but I'd gotten too many unexpected visitors of late and felt more comfortable with it close at hand.

"While you are interrogating your demon hunk about his goings on, you can ask him to help you find Ramiel. It's a win-win."

I rolled eyes at her description. For an ex-demon hunter, she didn't discriminate against them often. If they were hot they were hot. Didn't matter if they were demon, human, or otherwise. I think she'd just had too many blows to the head to be able to tell the difference.

"A win-win for me maybe, but he is likely to want something in return. Demons always do."

"So?" Adara snickered, "I'm sure there are several things he'd be interested in. In fact, there is one that you can borrow

called the Texas tongue twister that will —
"

"Good night, Adara," I cut her off before she could go into any further detail.

"Wait, what about the Georgia neck tickler—" I hung up the phone before she could finish her sentence, and then laughed. That woman.

She had a point though. Ramiel was bound and determined not to be found. I was running out of options. If I wanted to find him I'd have to break one of my solemn oaths.

Never make deals with demons.

7

"HOLY CRAP!" TRISHA SCREAMED holding on to the handle above her seat, "Ease up on the clutch, Mare!"

"I am," I ground my teeth as I shifted the gear stick and then car sputtered and stalled.

"Great you killed it," Trisha griped next to me gestured at the dashboard, "I thought you said you learned how to drive?"

"I did. I can't help that your car is so complicated," I crinkled my nose in distaste.

After much deliberation, I'd decided to let Trisha know about my newfound skill. I had liked what I'd experienced in Sid's truck so it only made sense that I would feel the same way about any other vehicle. Who knew, I might get my own one day.

But apparently, not all vehicles were the same. Trisha had been ecstatic about not having to drive me around anymore and promptly made me prove my skills. I might have to practice some more before investing in my own.

"That's because it's a stick shift," Trisha sighed and opened her door, "Let me drive. At this rate, it'll take until midnight before we get there."

I switched seats with Trisha and frowned. I didn't plan on letting a little thing like a stick shift deter me. I would learn how to drive if it killed me and then I could go on late night hunts without wasting so much money on taxis. Or getting Trisha in trouble with her parents.

"So, why am I going with you again?" Trisha asked as she adjusted the seat to fit her short stature, "If you're supposed to be asking for a favor, shouldn't you do that on your own?"

"What? You want to stay at the office and file paperwork?" I cocked a brow at her as she wrinkled her nose causing the skin around her eyes to bunch up. I never knew why she wore so much makeup. She said it was her way of expressing herself. I just thought she looked like she needed more sleep.

"Fine. I'll be your buffer," when I opened my mouth to argue the fact she held a finger up, "Uh uh, don't even try to deny it. You know as well as I do that I'm your buffer. You don't want to see Sid by yourself, so want me to be there in case things get heated."

I shrugged. I couldn't argue. She was right.

While my last meeting with Sid had ended alright. I still didn't like how I felt around him. At least, with Trisha there, he might keep his demonic powers under wraps.

Adara had gotten back to me early today with no new prospects but had said she'd keep checking. Since I was getting nowhere on my own, I'd finally decided to give in and ask for help from the demonic realm. I just hoped they didn't ask for too much in return.

"So, we get to the bar and what?" Trisha asked as she started down the road once more, "You use your feminine wiles to charm him into telling you what you want to know?" she snorted and giggled while muttering under her breath, "feminine wiles. Mary Wiles."

"Ha. Ha. Very funny," I retorted, crossing my arms over my chest, "I've thought about beating it out of him, to be honest."

"No," Trisha gasped, "Not Sid. He's too pretty to beat up. Can't you...you know, pay him."

I shot her a glare.

"Oh, right. Broke," she pulled her lip in between her teeth as she pondered on the issue, "You could offer him some information in exchange?"

"Like what? How to get blood out of a white shirt?" I scoffed, "I haven't been in heaven for over five years. Any information I once had is good and useless now."

"Well, I'm out of options. And we're here."

I glanced out the window as she put the car in park. The Night Owl. Once upon a time, I'd felt excited and maybe even a bit giddy about coming here. Because that meant I got to see Sid. Now my stomach fluttered and made me feel like I was going to be sick. Nervous? Who me?

When we stepped out of the bright light of the sidewalk and into the dimly lit bar, there was a moment where I was blind. I never understood why he kept his bar so badly lit. To hide the demons who occupied it? Or maybe there were worse things going on there that I didn't want to know about? Either way, it always screwed with my eyes.

"Come on," I walked up to the bar with Trisha close to my side. When I approached it, I was surprised to find that Sid wasn't working the counter. A muscled dark-skinned man served drinks to the single customer there—surprising considering it was just after one in the afternoon.

Once he noticed we were standing there he moved over to our side. With both hands on the counter, he glanced at me and then at Trisha and asked, "I.D."

"We aren't drinking," I stated and tried to look around the man, "I'm looking for Sidney."

The man wiped his hands off on a towel and jerked his head toward the back, "The boss is in the back right now. Is he expecting you?" his dark eyes stared at Trisha like he wondered what she tasted like.

Trisha moved a bit closer to my side and I didn't blame her. I shifted my leather jacket, flashing my gun to him causing him to jerk back.

"Look, just tell him Mary needs to talk to him, okay? We don't want any trouble."

This made the guy throw back his head and laugh a full-throated laugh. "You're funny, Miss Mary, but I'll relay your message," he glanced at Trisha once more before turning to do just that.

"Well, that was creepy," Trisha said.

"Yeah, you get those here," I remarked before glancing down at her. Her hands wrung in front of her, and she shifted from foot to foot, "Are you going to be okay? I won't let anything happen to you."

"Yeah, well, look what happened last time," she bit out before her eyes widened. Ouch. That stung a bit, "Oh, Mary. I'm sorry. I didn't mean that. I know it wasn't your fault or anything. I'm just a bit skittish around demons after the whole almost-getting-sacrificed gig."

"No, you're right," I shook my head, "I didn't protect you last time. I'll die before I let anything like that happen to you again."

"Maybe I wouldn't be such a liability if I learned how to use a gun?" she offered, and as the bartender came back I answered, "We'll see."

"The boss will be out in a second. Can I get you ladies something to drink?" his eyes once more on my young assistant. The hunger in his eyes made me gave me the feeling he was thinking more of having a drink himself than serving them. I bet he was a vampire, or some similar kind of leech.

"We're good," I answered shooting him a warning look.

Thankfully, we didn't have to wait long. Sid came out of the back office followed by a busty redhead. She smiled up at him and pecked him on the cheek which he returned with a tight smile. The redhead stalked out of the bar on her stiletto heels, her short skirt barely covering her backside.

I didn't know why but anger filled me. Just the sight of the woman, someone I had never met before, sent an uncontrollable rage through me. Why? She had never done anything to me. Could the very fact that she had been with Sid be it?

No. It didn't make sense. We had no claim over each other. We'd only kissed the one time. I had no reason to care what, or who, he did.

Still, even though I rationalized it with myself when Sid came over to us, I couldn't help but blurt out, "I hope you aren't using your powers on innocent humans."

The confusion on his face at my sudden anger only settled briefly before his gaze hardened, "What I do isn't your business."

Taken aback, I grabbed the edge of the counter and leaned in until I was so close I may just as well have been on the other side of the bar with him, "It is if you are hurting people. Don't make me have to put you down."

The bartender gave Sid and me a nervous look before he stepped away and pretended to clean off some glasses. Smart demon.

"You know, I'm getting tired of your threats. Either kill me, or don't. All this teasing is exhausting," Sid stood and came up to the other side of the bar.

"If you want to die so badly, maybe I just will." My hand itched to grab my gun and put a bullet through his head. The rational side of me was wondering what the hell was wrong with me while the other side just wanted to see him hurt. Like he had hurt me.

"Come on, kids," Trisha stepped up next to me and slid onto a bar stool, "Let's play nice."

"I will if she will," Sid let go of the bar and leaned back against the far counter, his arms crossed over his chest. Even in my anger my eyes still lingered on how nice his biceps looked beneath his shirt. The fact that I'd noticed irritated me even more.

"Fine," I ground out, my eyes never leaving Sid's face.

"Fine," Sid replied and then proceeded to stare me down, as if daring me to look away first.

After a moment or so, Trisha cleared her throat, "While watching you two glare at each other is fun and all, some of us have other places to be. Can we get this moving please?"

"Get what moving?" Sid asked dropping his arms and turning his attention to Trisha.

A childish part of me cheered. He'd yielded first. It didn't matter in the grand scheme of things, but it was the little wins that you had to hold on to.

"Mary," Trisha pushed me on the shoulder, forcing me to look to her, "Wasn't there something you wanted to ask Sid?"

Scowling down at my assistant, I didn't feel like asking for a favor now that I had threatened him. To be honest, I didn't want to be here at all.

"Come on, Mare. Just ask him," Trisha gave me a little nudge which made me growl slightly. She just rolled her eyes at me and tapped her black painted fingernails on the counter, "Go ahead, take as long as you want. I get paid by the hour."

I turned my attention from my assistant and then to Sid, but before I could ask my question the dark bartender drew my attention again. "When did you hire someone new?"

Obviously caught off guard by my question, Sid's eyebrows furrowed in confusion. His gaze then followed mine and he said, "Carl's not new."

"I've never seen him before," I countered.

"You don't come in all the time and it's *my* bar. I can do what I want with my employees. Carl just so happened to want some extra hours and I obliged."

"Because you are too busy stealing things for your dad, right?" I couldn't help but point out.

"If you'd stayed around long enough the other day, you would have found out."

The smirk on his face had to be illegal. It made my stomach flutter and gave me the sudden urge to smack him. Sure, I had taken off pretty fast after dropping him at the church. Especially when I had specifically gone in after him to grill him about his breaking and entering. But could anyone really blame me? There was too much attraction between us and it was hard to tell what was real and what was just his demon powers. No matter how much he says he has never used them on me.

"Well, I'm here now," I lifted my hands and glanced around, "You can tell me now."

"Nah-uh," he shook his head, "You had your chance. I'm going to keep my secrets secret for now," he locked eyes with me, the message in them talking about more than just his felony. But before I could ask him, he cleared his throat and fiddled with a few glasses in front of him, "So, did you just come here to ask me about my new bartender or was there another reason for your visit?"

"Yeah, Mare, stop beating around the bush and just ask him already. This back and forth, while entertaining, is giving me a headache," Trisha clutched her head.

She wasn't the only one.

Taking a deep breath, I prepared myself for the possibility that he would say no, or worse say yes, and want something I didn't want to give.

"I need your help," I said quickly. Apparently, fast enough that Sid's face scrunched in confusion and then a slow grin spread across his face. Damn him.

"So, the great Mary Wiles, needs help from little ole me?" he placed a hand on his chest with fake modesty, "I thought you didn't take help, especially from demons. I believe those were your words."

"Well, things change," I growled.

"You're telling me," Sid moved over to the bar and leaned on his elbows, his grin still on his face, "So, tell me. What can I do for you?"

Not letting his arrogance bother me anymore, I decided to just get it over with, "I need you to ask your demon friends about an archangel. He would have been taken about five years ago around the San Diego Valley. He might still be in captivity, or he could have gotten away."

"An archangel you say?" Sid rubbed his chin in thought, "I can't say that I've heard of any other angels except for yourself. What's his name?"

"Ramiel," the sudden clouds that covered Sid's eyes at the mention of Ramiel's name was not comforting, "Have you heard of him?"

"Yeah, I've heard of him," his tone had changed from teasing to dark. But I was too caught up in the possibility that he knew Ramiel to bother asking about it.

"Well then? Do you know where he is? Can you get him a message for me?" the questions poured out of my mouth in quick succession.

"No, I don't know where he is, but I know someone who does," his words were reluctant and still filled with anger.

"Then tell me who and I'll ask them," I pushed aside his discomfort in lieu of finding out more about my commander. The excitement that built in me was like nothing I'd ever felt. I was finally getting somewhere. I could find Ramiel after all.

When Sid didn't immediately answer, I frowned, "I don't have all day. Just spit it out already."

"Fine. You want to find your precious archangel?" Sid dropped his hands on the bar, both palms pounding the wood. The sound startled his one customer, but he didn't pay the man any mind. His eyes on me, Sid ground out, "Ask my father."

8

OF COURSE, THE ONE person who could help me find Ramiel was the one I had just helped stop from crossing over to the human world. If that wasn't ironic, I didn't know what was.

Trisha drove us back to the office. Neither one of us had the patience to deal with my driving. The ride was quiet, each of us in our own thoughts. I didn't know what Trisha was thinking but I knew my mind was reeling.

Sid had told us that he'd send a message to his father and then he would get in contact with me when Asmodeus was available. The fact that Sid could easily contact his father meant that I hadn't gotten rid of Asmodeus for good. Not that I'd believed I had. Demon lords were far stronger than the average demon.

It also meant that Asmodeus was back in the human world. Presumably, possessing another helpless innocent. Just the thought of having to deal with him made my blood boil. He'd killed several young women, the last time he had tried to cross over to the human world, and had almost murdered Trisha. I couldn't see anything good coming from talking to him. He'd be lucky if I didn't put another holy bullet in his brain first. If he would even meet with me.

"We're here," Trisha said in a small voice that had me glancing at her with concern. Her eyes were fixed in front of her, her naturally pale skin even paler, her usual chipper disposition completely shadowed by something in her eyes. That's when I noticed the dark circles she had been trying to hide beneath her makeup. Her face was slightly thinner and her hands gripped the stirring wheel until her knuckles changed colors.

"Trisha," I said as I began to move toward her, "Why don't you take some time off? I can deal with Asmodeus on my own. There's no need for you to put yourself in danger."

Trisha's gaze turned to mine and her lips ticked up in a forced grin, "Like I could let you have all the fun. If I get the chance, I want a piece of that asshole."

Shaking my head, I placed my hand on her arm, "I'm all for kicking demon butt but not at the cost of your health. Don't waste your life looking for revenge."

"You're one to talk," Trisha snapped, her eyes narrowing, "All you've done since you got here was try to get revenge on those demons who hurt you." When I tried to argue she put her hand up, "Now, I might have only found out about your angelic heritage a month ago but don't think I haven't noticed the jobs you take. Anything that has to do with demons and you are on it. Especially, if it means you get to hurt someone. You don't go out. You spend all your time working. Even that delicious specimen Sid can't break through your walls."

"He's a demon."

"Half-demon," Trisha pointed out, "And you didn't even know until recently. Before that, you were slowly starting to figure out your feelings for him. And don't even try to deny it. We both know you had, and still have, feelings for him. You're just hurt right now because he lied to you. Even an idiot could tell by the way you guys went at each other back there."

"But I—"

"Get out," Trisha snapped cutting me off, "I'm off the clock and you have a call to wait for."

I clamped my mouth shut and pursed my lips. Trisha's eyes moved back to the front staring at whatever it was in her mind eating at her. I didn't say anything else, just got out of the car and watched as she sped away.

My assistant was a tough one, that's for sure, but even the strong ones had their own darkness to fight. I knew from experience.

Moving passed Madame Serena's, I only briefly paused to notice she had closed early. I shrugged it off. She could do what she liked. Closing earlier didn't have to mean anything.

As I made my way up the stairs and to my office I began to feel increasingly tired. Rubbing my eyes, I dug around in my pocket for my keys. Maybe Trisha was right. I worked too much. Maybe I should find a hobby?

I turned the key in the door and twisted the handle all the while my mind reeling with different hobbies I could take up. I wasn't much for going to clubs. The last time I had gone hadn't ended well. Not really a night owl anyways.

Pulling my coat off, I walked across the reception area and to my office door. Opening the door, I wondered how hard it would be to get into fishing. I'd always loved the idea of providing for others. I could give them away to the needy but then again I'd have too much time alone with my thoughts.

"I have always enjoyed fishing myself."

My gun was out and pointed before I could even register who the voice belonged to. Hands in the air, a cocky grin on his face was a man I recognized as some actor who, by Trisha's account, was quickly rising up the ranks. Jake something.

Dark hair and piercing green eyes, he had a strong jaw line and a dimple in his right cheek. I'd have wondered how and why an actor would be in my office and seated in my desk chair, except for three things.

One the perfectly tailored suit encasing his body did not scream some Hollywood star. Two, his aura was so dark I was surprised I hadn't felt it from the front door. Three, I hadn't said the thing about fishing out loud.

"Asmodeus," I stated setting my coat down so I could hold my gun with both hands.

"Muriel," he rolled the r of my name making it sound more exotic than it was. Just the sound of my name on his lips pulled at something low in me. I bit the side of my cheek to force his influence back. I knew what this demon lord could do to an unsuspecting victim.

"What are you doing here?" I held the gun pointed at his head not letting up for a moment.

"Straight to the point. All you angels are alike," Asmodeus tapped a pen on my desk against the wood, "I'd always liked angels. I never understood why we were enemies."

"Probably because we don't kill people for fun," I snapped.

"Oh, we have much more in common than you think," Asmodeus countered and then frowned at the gun still pointed at his head, "Come now, I mean you no harm. Have a seat," he gestured to the chair I usually reserved for clients.

"You're in my seat." It was childish, sure, but he had come in unannounced not the other way around. Besides, it was taking everything I had in me not to blow his head off right there.

Sadly, my words only caused him to smile, his eyes crinkling and his dimple deepening, "Well, I'm sure you can live without it for a few moments."

I stood there for a moment, my gun still pointed and starting to feel foolish. One really shouldn't point a gun unless they mean to pull the trigger, otherwise it just looks silly. Finally, after a moment or two, I conceded. I slowly dropped my arm, but didn't holster the weapon.

I sat down at one of the chairs in front of him and crossed one leg over the other, my hand holding my gun sitting in my lap, "Alright, talk."

Asmodeus tut-tutted at me, "You can't even put that thing away?"

Teeth grinding, I said, "This is the best you are going to get. You're lucky you're still breathing."

The demon in front of me shook his head and frowned, "And here I thought you wanted my help."

I stared at him for a moment. Was this guy serious? "You broke into my home and not too long ago tried to kill me and my best friend. You'll forgive me if I'm a little cautious."

"Bah," Asmodeus scoffed, "That was so long ago. This is the here and now. I've long since given up on crossing to this world by sacrificial means," he smiled at me, his hands open wide as if to say, look how innocent I am, "We are on the same side now. There is no need for threats."

"We'll never be on the same side. Not as long as you are a demon who hurts people," I shook my head but put my gun in its holster. I didn't clip it or put the safety on—I wasn't that stupid.

"There now. Was that so hard?" he cocked his head to the side and I had a sudden urge to pull the gun back out and just shoot him. Surely there was another way to find Ramiel?

"I put the gun away, now tell me where Ramiel is." My patience was wearing thin. I knew the longer this little meeting went on, the more likely one of us would end up bloody or dead. I was determined it wouldn't be me.

"Now, why would I tell you that?"

That was it. I was shooting him. I didn't care if he knew where Ramiel was or if I never found my commander. I could not stand to look at his grinning face for a moment longer.

Before my hand could reach for my gun, Asmodeus was up from his chair and held my hand in his steel grasp, "Forgive me. I cannot seem to help myself. There just something about you that makes me want to tease and taunt. Probably why my son is so infatuated with you. There's no need to get violent."

Ignoring, his reference to Sid, I pulled my hand out of his grasp and leaned back from him, "Funny coming from a demon."

Asmodeus moved away from me to lean back against the edge of the desk, "You don't know everything about us, Mary. Not all of us kill just for the sake of killing.

Many of us upper beings only kill when it serves a certain purpose."

"It's still killing."

He frowned and crossed his arms over his chest in a way that reminded me of Sid, "But you kill just as much as we do. You've killed dozens of humans in your quest for vengeance."

"They were possessed by demons," I argued.

"But you didn't have to kill them. You could have dispossessed them just as easily. But instead, you chose the more violent approach because it made you feel good."

Shaking my head, I started to say no but stopped. He was right in a way. I could have dispossessed those I had killed without a second thought. But each removal takes so much energy it was just easy to kill the host when I knew the likelihood of them being alive was low. Didn't make it any better.

"See," Asmodeus pointed at me, "you know I'm right. We aren't so different after all."

"So, what? Now we get to have slumber parties and talk about our favorite kills?" I snarled.

"Oh, that does sound like fun. But I think we both know why we are really here," he smiled at me knowingly, "You wish to have your friend back and I can help you find him. Though, why you would want some archangel instead of my dear boy is beyond me. I'm sure Sidney is a lot better of a lover than some stuck up angel."

"Sidney isn't my anything."

"Oh?" he cocked a brow at me, "I was under the impression that you two were," he pressed his hands together and when I only glared he shrugged, "Oh, well. No harm done then."

He patted his hands on his thighs and clicked his tongue, "Anyways, back to your friend. Ramiel is it?"

"Yes," I relaxed a bit now that we were finally getting to the point, "He would have been captured right before I was. He contacted me while I was in the hospital, but I haven't been able to track him down."

"Oh, you were in the hospital?" Asmodeus made a cooing noise. "If I'd known I'd have sent flowers."

I glared at him, "I was in the hospital getting stitched up from a wound you inflicted when you skewered me."

"Oh, yes. I did do that. Apologies. I have quite a temper," he waved his hand in the air as if it was an everyday thing to stab someone. For all, I knew it probably was for him.

"Anyways," I bit out. It was like pulling teeth to get anywhere with this guy, "Ramiel would have been taken a little more than five years ago. He contacted me last month so he has to be in the city somewhere."

"Have you ever thought that maybe he doesn't want to be found?" Asmodeus asked with a raised brow, "Maybe his little message was meant to soothe your tortured soul and not to make a connection."

"I don't have a soul," I snapped, "And neither do you. So stop with the sympathy act. Either you can help me find him, or not. If not, we are wasting time that I could have used to find him."

"Now, don't get fussy. I'm trying to give you all the possibilities . . . you know . . . as your friend," he smiled at me.

"Let's get one thing clear," I stood so that I was almost nose to nose with him, "We might have to work together, but we are not, and never will be, friends. And the first chance I get I'll blast you back to hell where you belong."

My threat only made him smile in delight. Either I needed to work on my intimidation methods or he was just one tough nut to crack. Either way, I hated to waste a good threat and before he could see me move, I shot my fist out and smashed into the side of his face.

Asmodeus's, or rather the face of the human he was wearing, jerked to the side. Blood trickled from his nose and I smirked.

"Do we have an understanding?" I asked sweetly, stepping back from him.

He reached up and touched the blood, his lips curling up. He chuckled as he pulled out a silk handkerchief and dabbed at his nose, "Yes, I believe we do."

"Good. Now, let me know when you find something out about Ramiel," I turned from him and stared over at my fold-out couch which was still undone from this morning, "You know where to find me."

Clearly dismissed, Asmodeus didn't take the hint. Instead he cleared his throat. Spinning back around, I placed my hands on my hips and sighed. "What do you want now?"

"It's not what I want. It's what you want. I will find your angel. If he is to be found. But I want something in exchange."

"Of course, you do," I threw my hands up in the air, "What do you want? Five new virgins for your ritual? 'Cause I won't hand anyone over to you to be slaughtered."

"Oh no, no," he shook his head and laughed, "Nothing so crude."

"Then what is it?"

His eyes lit with a hunger that I had never seen before and he said, "Michael's blade."

9

"WHAT ARE YOU GOING to do with it?" I asked not believing my ears.

Michael's blade was lost hundreds of years ago. It had supposedly been seen during the second world war, but no one knew for certain. How it even got down on earth was beyond me.

"That's not really your concern now, is it?" Asmodeus responded, "You want your angel, and I want the blade of Michael. That's the deal."

Pursing my lips together, I growled, "Even if I felt comfortable getting it for you, I wouldn't even know where to begin to find it."

"I've got that covered as well," Asmodeus reached into his coat pocket and drew out a piece of paper.

I took the paper from him and glanced down at it. The address wasn't somewhere I recognized, but that didn't mean anything.

"That's the address of where it is currently located," Asmodeus continued, "You might ask my son for a tip or two about how to get in. I believe he has already botched his attempt at retrieving it for me."

"This was what he got arrested for?" I shook the piece of paper in the air, "Trying to get you the blade?"

Asmodeus sniffed, "My son is loyal to me. The majority of the time. Why wouldn't he risk everything to help me?"

"Help you do what exactly?" I raised a brow at him.

"You'll find out soon enough," he adjusted his cufflinks, "Get the blade and I'll get your angel. Then we can discuss the particulars. Now, if you would excuse me, this human host sure wears one out."

He was gone and out my door before I could ask him anymore. Glaring down at the paper in my hand, I was tempted to burn it.

I didn't know what Asmodeus wanted with Michael's blade but whatever it was, it wasn't good. Was it worth seeing Ramiel again on the off chance that Asmodeus was up to no good? The answer was cloudy and I didn't like it.

After making sure my office was locked up tight, I collapsed onto my bed. This day just kept getting better and better.

Not only was I a private detective, and by Asmodeus's definition a murderer. Now, I was a thief. I wasn't under any impression that I could just waltz in there and ask for the blade. Even if they really had it. Trisha was just going to love this.

The thought of my young assistant made me frown harder. I hadn't noticed how affected she had been by her encounter with Asmodeus. I forgot sometimes that she's still human, and not more than a child at that. I'd have to be more mindful in the future. I'd hate to be responsible for one more soul being damned because of my actions. Even if just by association.

"OUCH, MOVE OVER," TRISHA pushed at my shoulder as we tried to unsuccessfully to move quietly along the backside of the mansion before us.

The address had led us to a large estate that belonged to some big shot collector. The house was owned under the name A. Hunter. What the A stood for even Trisha couldn't find out.

When I had explained Trisha about our new job she had jumped up and down for joy, but when I'd told her who it was for her face had fallen.

"Are you sure this is a good idea?" Trisha whispered to me for the millionth time, "We don't even know what he is going to do with it. He could turn around and stab you with it for all we know."

I paused in my surveillance of the house, "It's not that kind of blade."

"What kind of blade is it then? Most blades are sharp, which means they can cut stuff. Meaning you," she pointed a gloved finger at me.

One part of the mission she couldn't hold back her enthusiasm for was our outfits. Decked out in black pants and long sleeve shirts, Trisha had even gotten us black gloves and knitted caps, "To hide our hair," though the way she had her black and pink hair styled, the hat really wasn't going to help any.

"The blade of Michael isn't really a weapon," I explained as I came to stop next to a window.

Getting passed the guards had been easy enough. There were large green bushes that lined the whole left side of the gate. After some scratches and some not-so-pleasant words from Trisha, we'd crawled our way to the other side of those bushes and over the metal gate.

Now, I had to find a way into the house without setting off some kind of alarm. Luckily, I had Trisha for that.

"Will this one work?" I asked, pointing to the window that was covered by a heavy curtain.

Trisha glanced into the window and down at something I couldn't see, "Yeah, that'll work. Now, if you could just break the glass, I can get my wires in there to disable the alarm and then we can open the window without worry."

I had called up Sid after his father left and found out the details of his capture. Apparently, the house was rigged with security alarms on the windows. Something he had been lax in finding out beforehand. I wouldn't make the same mistake.

"Okay, hold on," I pulled out a knife I had tucked into a sheath along my thigh. Using it to cut open the screen covering the window, I eased the edges open. Once the screen was open enough to pop it out, I placed my hands on the edge of the window's frame. Trying to hold back some of my strength, I hit the window with my glove-covered hand. The window shattered louder than I had expected and I winced.

"Shhh," Trisha whispered harshly.

We both waited for a moment, my heart beat loudly in my chest and my breath held. After a moment, when no one came running, I let the breath out and moved out of the way for Trisha to do her magic.

"Alright, all done," Trisha clapped her hands together after a few minutes. "Now, just pop the window open and we are good to go."

I grabbed the frame of the window and gave it a shove up. We waited briefly for an alarm to go off once the window was fully opened. When nothing went off, I proceeded into the mansion.

Glass cracked beneath my booted feet and I tried to get around it with as little noise as possible in the dim light. With Trisha at my back, I made my way into the darkened room. The room we had picked was a bedroom. An unoccupied one, by the way, the bed was made and there was dust on the dressers and side tables.

"You'd think for rich people they'd keep their stuff clean," Trisha commented from behind me.

"Well, we aren't here to critique their housekeeping. Let's just get the blade and get out of here," I gestured for her to follow me as I crept over to the door.

I held my hand up for her to stop but apparently, Trisha wasn't paying attention because she bumped into my back. I glared over my shoulder at her.

"Sorry," she whispered, her shoulders by her ears.

Pursing my lips, I turned back to the door. I reached out and twisted the door handle and slowly eased it open. When the door was open far enough, I poked my head out and glanced around. The hallway outside of the room was as dark as the inside and there were no guards in sight.

"Come on," I waved her forward as I inched out of the room.

The house was quiet. No movement or hint that someone even lived there. Which just made my job easier.

When we arrived at the end of the hallway we turned into a large open room. In this room, were dozens of large displays each encased in a glass box.

"Wow," Trisha whispered, "They weren't kidding when they said they were a collector."

I nodded my head but didn't answer. They could have hundreds of items but I only cared about one.

We moved through the displays searching for the blade. I briefly noticed a few items that shouldn't have been there. A copy of the original Book of Enoch. A golden chalice that suspiciously resembled one from our crystal lake in heaven that had been lost before the middle ages. There was even a case with some feathers that I recognized as those of an angel. Not an archangel by any means, but an angel none the less. Whoever this collector was they knew their celestial artifacts.

"Mary," Trisha called out to me in a whisper, "Is this it?"

I moved across the marble floor as quickly as I could without making a sound, and stopped at Trisha's side. The case before her was larger than the rest. Inside, on a tall wooden stand sat a blade no longer than my thigh. The hilt was made of bronze with a clear crystal at the end, and the blade itself was engraved with a language no human would ever hear.

"What's it say?" Trisha asked.

"The road will open to those who are worthy," I replied, my lips pressed into a thin line. I didn't mention to her that it also said, "And the path to hell for those who are not." No need to get her hackles up anymore.

Now that we found what we were looking for, I reached up to grab the glass case off of it. But just as my hand touched the cool surface a high-pitched squeal filled my ears. Trisha grabbed her head and fell to the ground groaning in agony.

The noise was irritating but not unbearable. At least, not to me. Shaking off the sound, I smashed my hand into the glass, shattering the case. No need to be subtle now.

Grabbing the handle of the blade, I reached over and pulled Trisha up by her arm, "We've gotta go!" I yelled over the alarm, followed by what I could only assume was the guards hollering from somewhere else in the mansion.

I dragged Trisha, who was still clutching her head, out of the showroom and back toward the way we'd come. The front doors of the showroom burst open and half a dozen uniformed men spilled into the room. Everyone froze. They stared at us, while Trisha and I stared at them.

The markings on their clothing were familiar but I couldn't quite place them. They seemed surprised that the intruders were two women but after a moment, they seemed to shake it off and one of them called out, "Get them!"

Taking it as my cue to make a run for it, I darted into the hallway we had come down earlier. With Trisha trailing behind me, I turned to tell her to hurry and ran smack into a hard surface.

Falling to the ground, my face ached and felt like ping pongs being batted around in my head. Groaning, I glanced up to see what I had run into.

A door.

Someone had opened a door right in front of me and in my distracted state I had run straight into it. When Asmodeus asked me why I'd failed I'd have to tell him I was defeated by a piece of wood. How lame was that?

I pushed up on my elbows, prepared to grab Trisha and run when I realized my hand was empty. I searched around for the blade I had gone to all the trouble to steal and then spotted it a few feet away right next to a pair of boots that had just appeared out of the formidable door.

My eyes trailed up the boot and to the black leggings, over the baggy purple shirt that hung off one shoulder. And to Adara's smirking face.

"Well, look what the demons dragged in."

10

I SAT AT THE breakfast bar in the kitchen of the house we'd just failed to rob, with a pack of ice pressed against my face. I winced at the cold touch of the ice on my sore face. Reminder to self: don't get hit by doors.

Once Adara had realized who had broken in she had called off the guards who were other members of her hunter's guild.

"You know," Adara said from the kitchen sink as she washed dishes. Her dark hair fell down her back in waves and almost brushed the top of her hips. The tank top she wore exposed her muscled arms and the tips of a tattoo of a phoenix currently hidden behind her hair. I rarely ever saw it uncovered. "You're lucky you ran into me. It could have ended so much worse for you."

"Ran into her, ha! Do you get it?" Trisha giggled and nudged me in the side.

I grimaced, "Yes, very humorous."

"No, really," Adara's face turned serious as she spun away from the sink, "This is the Phoenix Hunter's Guild. If you had been a demon you'd have lost your head before you crossed the threshold."

"Lucky for me then that I'm not a demon," I answered bitterly. Sitting there now, I didn't feel so lucky. Freaking Trisha didn't have a scratch on her. Then again *I* was the one who had walked into a damn door.

"Well, you got the security part right on," Trisha commented, wiggling a finger in her ear, "I thought I was going to go deaf."

"That alarm is meant to incapacitate any living being, human or otherworldly," Adara placed her hands on the other side of the bar and looked to me, "Apparently, it needs to be adjusted if it doesn't affect angelic beings the same way."

I shrugged. "Sorry?"

"Still," Adara watched me closely, searching for something in my face, "The fact that it didn't is worrying. Can't have just anyone waltzing in here. As you saw we have several artifacts that I could imagine an angel or two would love to get their hands on," Her dark eyes settled on the blade that sat on the table between us.

"How did you get all of these anyways?" I reached to pick up the blade but Adara shot out a hand and scooped it up before I could touch it.

"No touching until you tell me what's going on," she waved the blade in the air, "And the guild has many connections. Most of these have been here since I was a child."

"You know," Trisha jumped in before I could explain what we were doing there, "For someone who works at a bar, you sure are loaded."

Adara rolled her eyes, her lips twisting, "This isn't *my* house. It's the guild's. Or rather my father's house."

We all have our demons. Adara's just happened to be dead.

Once upon a time, Adara was one of the most revered of all the Phoenix demon hunters. Her father, the head of the guild, could not have been prouder or more thrilled to have such a successor. That was until Adara fell in love with one of the creatures she had sworn to kill.

When her father found out he had demanded she kill her lover, but when Adara refused her father killed him right in front of her. Adara retired after that swearing never to hunt demons again but she did help me on occasion, which I think made her feel like she wasn't completely shirking her calling.

"But still," Trisha whistled and turned around her seat, "This place is nice. I don't know why you bother working at that run-down bar when you could live in a place like this."

Adara snapped a hand towel at Trisha causing her to scowl, "I work there because I like it. I might not kill demons anymore but there are plenty of other reasons to hunt them that don't involve blood. Or," she smirked a bit, "not too much anyways."

Trisha's lips curled down in disgust and I frowned.

Adara was one of my best friends and all, but I didn't understand how she could lie with someone who used to be her enemy. In my book, all demons were bad. They were just created that way, and trying to make them into something good was like asking a tiger to change its stripes.

I did think that Adara partially screwed around with demons-vampires particularly—as a way to piss off her father. Each notch in her bedpost was one more mark on his precious heir. She would never be the leader of the guild—at least not if she or her father had anything to say about it.

"What are you doing here anyways? I thought you didn't have anything to do with these guys?" I gestured around the kitchen as if the other guild members were right there.

"I do come by sometimes," Adara explained, "Just not unless . . ."

"You're stinking drunk," I supplied for her.

She gave a small laugh and scratched the back of her head, "You got me. This place is closer than my apartment so sometimes when I get too carried away, I like to crash in my old room. Good thing too, or you guys would have been mincemeat. Well, maybe not you," she pointed at Trisha, "but definitely you," Adara turned back to me, finger now aiming at my chest"

"That would be interesting to see," Trisha smiled bouncing in her seat slightly, "You heal really fast, so if you lost an arm, or even a finger, would it come crawling back and reattach itself? Or maybe it grows back! Like in the comics!"

"See what you've started?" I glared at Adara—who only grinned—before I turned to Trisha, "No. If I lose a finger it won't grow back, otherwise my wings would have come back on their own years ago."

Talking about my wings made me wince and my hands itched to touch the scars. I dug my fingernails into my palms to keep them from doing just that. Adara shared my frown and almost reached out to comfort me, but I shook my head making her drop her hand. Talking about it only made it worse, and I didn't need any flashbacks right now.

"And as far as reattaching itself, I don't know. I've never tried it," I shrugged, "And don't plan on it," I snapped when Trisha opened her mouth.

She crossed her arms over her chest and pouted, "Party pooper."

"So anyways," Adara drew out turning her attention from the pouting girl to me, "We've stalled enough. What are you doing here? And don't give me that client confidentiality bullshit," she held a finger up in warning at me when I started to answer.

"I wasn't," I said, "I was going to say that it was a demon thing and you shouldn't worry about it."

"All the more reason I should know," Adara leaned forward on the bar, crossing her arms in front of her, the blade close to her chest, "The guild is kindly letting me handle this because you are my friends. Otherwise, you would be in the basement being tortured for information. So, if it has to do with demons, the guild will want to know about it."

"Not this demon," I shook my head, "This isn't someone they can just go waltzing off to chop his head off or put a stake through his heart."

"We deal in more than vampires, Mary."

I pursed my lips. She just didn't get it. Humans never did. And neither did the guild members even though they were hardly human with their increased strength and speed. Not to forget their ability to spew fire from their body—though not all of them had that ability, thank God. If Adara had such powers, she had never shown them to me, but as the future leader, or former future leader, of the guild, it was unlikely that she didn't have their most deadly ability.

"What are you thinking?" Adara cocked her head to the side as if she could read my mind, "What's got you so spooked?"

"I talked to Sid about Ramiel."

The kitchen was quiet as I waited for Adara to process my words. *She* had told me to ask him and now that I finally had, I wished I hadn't. Maybe it was better if Ramiel was never found. Especially if it meant dealing with demons.

But it was too late for that. I had made the deal and now I had to stick with it. If I backed out I could imagine quite a few things that Asmodeus could do in return. My eyes drifted over to Trisha and my face hardened. No matter what I wouldn't let him touch her again. Even if I had to go to hell myself and kill his ass.

"So what did he say?" Adara asked, caution in her voice.

"Well, they fought like an old married couple for a few minutes," Trisha said breaking the tension in the room, "And the sexual tension between those two, woo wee," she fanned herself, "Even *I* was getting hot and bothered by it."

"Trisha!" I scolded.

"What?" she held her hands up, "It's true. You guys just need to do it and get it over with. You'll feel so much better for it."

"Did I ever mention how much I like you?" Adara smirked. "We should hang out sometime. I could introduce you to some of my . . . friends."

"You," I pointed to Trisha, "stop. And you," I turned my attention to Adara, "She's underage and not helping."

"Sorry, sorry. Don't get your holy panties in a twist," Adara laughed. The mention of my undergarments reminded me of Sid and not in an unpleasant way.

126

Irritation filled me at the thought. Couldn't I do one thing without thinking of him? He betrayed me and lied to me. I should be thinking fully about Ramiel and getting him back not about the half-demon who made me feel . . . well, more than I had felt in my entire existence.

Licking my lips, I pushed the thought of Sid back and changed the subject, "Anyways, back to the point. We need that," I pointed to the blade Adara was still keeping close to her chest, "In exchange for Ramiel."

"So you found him?" Adara's eyes lit up.

"Not exactly."

"What's that supposed to mean?" Adara's dark brows furrowed.

I wasn't being coy for fun. There was a reason I didn't flat out tell her what I wanted it for. While Adara might be all gung-ho to screw her way through all of the demons in Los Angeles to get back at her dad, she was still a Phoenix hunter. It was in her blood to protect this world and I didn't think she would be particularly happy about me giving one of their rare artifacts to a demon. Even if they didn't want it for anything than just to have it. Which I wasn't stupid enough to think.

"It means," Trisha spoke up giving me an annoyed look, "That she is trading that for getting Asmodeus, the guy who almost killed me, to find Ramiel for her."

Adara made a disgusted sound and glared at me, "You don't even know if this guy has Ramiel and you are willing to break into the Phoenix Guild? You could have died!"

"I know! Okay, I know," I put the ice pack down and rubbed the sides of my head, "I didn't know . . . we didn't know that the mansion was yours. We were just going where Sid had failed to break into earlier."

This caused Adara's eyes to widen, "That was him?"

"Yeah, apparently the little breaking-and-entering incident I had to bail him out of was to try and steal that blade," I pointed at the artifact, "Now, since he failed, his father is having me get it in his place."

"How could you?" Adara burst out, unreasonably angry. She held the dagger up swinging it in the air as she started to pace, "Do you not care about humanity at all?"

"Of course, I do," My brows scrunched down at her ire. Why was she so mad? It was a stupid dagger. Not a bomb.

"Then why would you even think about giving Michael's blade to that monster?" Adara pointed the dagger at me causing me to lean back slightly.

"Wait, wait," Trisha held up her hands, "I'm confused. Why wouldn't we want to give that thing to Asmodeus? Besides the obvious fact that he's a demon lord?"

"No, reason. It's just a blade," I reached out and snatched the dagger from Adara before she could pull it back. Holding it by the hilt I held it up for Trisha to look at, "It might sound important but it's just a normal blade. Not even a very sharp one at that."

"Then why is it called Michael's blade? Shouldn't it like flame or something?" Trisha reached out and slid her finger along the smooth side of the blade, disappointment in her face when nothing happened.

I shrugged and put the blade down, "Michael is a blowhard. Thinks he's all high-and-mighty 'cause he's God's right-hand man ever since Lucifer fell. For all I know, he made up how important it was to make himself look better."

"You don't know, do you?" The disbelief in Adara's voice pulled my attention away from the dagger.

"Know what?" Trisha and I said at the same time.

"That dagger," Adara pointed at the blade in my hand, "isn't just some accessory. Now, I can't say that for myself whether or not it lights on fire, but I do know that it's not something you want to hand over to a demon lord, no matter the reason."

"Stop beating around the bush and just tell us already. What's so great about this piece of junk?" I looked over the blade, the inscription catching the light as I turned it around in my hands.

"You noticed the writing, didn't you?" Adara asked and then kept going, not waiting for my answer, "It's not just some pretty turn of phrase. That blade isn't used in battle. It's used to cut through space and time itself. As in creating portals."

"Portals?" Trisha asked, "Portals for what?"

This time it was me who answered, "Portals to hell. Or rather out of it."

11

THE CAR WAS SILENT as we made our way back to the office. After Adara had filled us in on what Michael's blade really did, I think both of us had a lot on our mind. I knew I did.

Who could have thought that Michael, that pompous arrogant ass, had a weapon that could create portals between hell and earth? The thought of a weapon that powerful in the hands of God's golden boy wasn't all that surprising. In his eyes, Michael could do no wrong, but to the rest of us he was nothing but a stuck up the-universe-revolves-around-me jerk.

He'd probably been too busy showing it off on earth and that's why it had gotten lost. It was only by luck that the Phoenix guild had gotten a hold of it and had known it for what it was. I couldn't imagine the chaos that would have ensued had it fallen into the wrong hands. We had enough of a demon problem, we didn't need hordes of them deciding to take a vacation in the human world.

"So, what are you going to do?" Trisha asked in a quiet voice as she parked the car outside of our building. The question was simple enough, but I knew what she was really asking.

I had left the dagger with Adara until we could figure out our next move. I wasn't going to take the chance of bringing that thing to my place in case I received another visit from the demon of lust himself. I figured if there was a reason Asmodeus hadn't gone for it himself then it wouldn't be safe anywhere else. For all I knew, Adara and her crew had some demon charm on the place. It would explain why he had tried to get Sid to steal it and not one of his other guys.

"I don't know yet," I answered and sighed, "I guess just wait and see if he keeps up his side of the deal and find out what he wants it for."

"What he wants it for?" Trisha exclaimed, "We know what he wants it for!"

"Now, we don't know for sure he wants to use it to come over to this world," I defended.

"Mary! Be more naive, why don't you?" Trisha screamed, "This is a demon lord. He just sacrificed virgins to try and cross over. What makes you think he doesn't want this blade for that very reason?"

"Fine. You're right. I'm being stupid," I ran a hand through my hair and growled when it caught on a tangle. Yanking my fingers through the knot, I winced as I pulled some of my hair out. This was so not my night.

"I don't know what to do." Leaning forward in my seat, I ran my hands over my face and then slammed my palms into the dashboard causing Trisha to jump in her seat. "Damn it. Why does everything have to be so complicated?"

"That's life, Mare," Trisha's small hand patted my back, "It's one hard decision after the other, and then we die."

"That's pretty morbid, Trish," I turned to look at her and she gave me a weak smile.

"Well, I don't wear black just because I like the color."

I smiled back at her and sighed again, "Alright, well. I guess I'll have to see what Asmodeus says and then go from there." When Trisha frowned, I grabbed her hand in mine and gave it a squeeze, "I won't let anything bad happen to you. I promise. I'll kill the asshole myself before I let him touch you."

"I know, Mare," Trisha squeezed my hand in return and then gave my shoulder a push, "Now get the hell out of my car, I'm already out passed curfew. My mom is going to kill me."

"Just tell her I'm paying you overtime," I suggested.

Trisha laughed, "You hardly pay me now, which by the way means you need to take on some of those other jobs. Can't save the world if you're living on the streets."

"True . . ." I dragged out. I knew she was right. I couldn't keep passing up on jobs because it was below me, or because it was not something I wanted to do. And I couldn't keep expecting Trisha to remain on what I paid her, or with what I didn't pay her at times.

"Alright," I nodded, "Tomorrow morning, we'll go over those messages again and we'll figure something out. Until then, go get some sleep."

"You got it, boss. I'll be here—" A crash followed by a scream from our building had both of us scrambling from the car.

We raced up the stairs and stopped at the already open office door. Trisha and I exchanged a look.

"I didn't leave it open." Trisha shook her head.

I gestured for Trisha to stand back behind me. I unholstered my gun clicking the safety off as I eased the door open.

The office was dark and there was no sign of an intruder. I sighed and flicked the light on just as a groan came from the room.

My gaze shot to a figure sprawled out on the ground by Trisha's desk. I held my hand up to Trisha to stop her from coming in any further as I inched toward the figure. The intruder groaned again and started to get up off the ground, a dark head coming into view.

Bouncy black curls.

"Gracie Lou," I clenched my teeth and lowered my gun. "What the hell are you doing here?"

Trisha rushed to the girl's side, helping her up from the floor. I closed the office door and locked it. When I turned around Gracie Lou and Trisha were seated at the couch.

Gracie Lou's face was puffy and red from crying. The innocent look on her face was marred by stark terror. A sinking feeling filled me and I dropped the veil on my powers.

The darkness I'd seen in her soul when I'd first met her had grown, and now swirled with an angry redness. It made my one hand tighten on my gun and my other reach for my talisman. I was afraid of this.

"Who did it for you?" I couldn't hold back the disgust in my voice.

"What?" Trisha's shocked expression reached my eyes. "What are you talking about, Mary?"

"You were right," Gracie Lou's small voice quaked, "I should have listened to you. Found some other way to get back at them."

"That's right. You should have," I snapped, earning me a warning look from Trisha, which I ignored. "Now tell me who did it for you?"

"No one," she shook her head, "I joined a forum about demons. I asked around about how to go about summoning one and a guy on there directed me to this book I could get at any local bookstore," Gracie Lou shrugged, "I didn't put much stock in it. I thought I'd get it and check it out," her eyes turned from my unfeeling glare to Trisha who patted her hand, "I didn't think anything would come of it. That it would just be something fun to do, make myself feel better."

"Gracie Lou," Trisha glanced up at me and then back to her, "What did you do?"

She broke down then. Tears poured out of her eyes and wracking sobs caused her to hiccup. It went on for a few minutes as Trisha sat beside her, rubbing her back in circles.

"It was just a spell. Some silly words," Gracie Lou sniffled, "I didn't think anything would happen."

"But something did happen, didn't it?" I probed.

"Yes," Gracie Lou breathed out, "something terrible."

I let out an aggravated growl. That was the problem with humans. They didn't think. They thought it was just all fun and games. They never thought of the consequences.

Before I could chastise Gracie Lou for going and taking matters into her own hands, she started crying again.

Between each sob, she said, "Blood. There was so much blood," her dark curls shook back and forth, "I didn't want to hurt them. Just scare them. But I couldn't stop it."

"Gracie Lou," I holstered my gun and knelt in front of her, grabbing her by the shoulders, "What did you do?"

Her eyes met mine and the darkness there reflected back. The terror on her face changed as her lips curled into a devastating grin.

"I killed them. All of them," she threw her head back and laughed. I let go of Gracie Lou as her touch burned.

"Trisha get away from her," I ordered, my eyes not leaving the girl in front of me.

Trisha jumped off the couch and stumbled to my side, her hands clutching my arm.

"What the hell is wrong with her?" Trisha whispered. I could feel the fear in her as her fingers dug into my arm.

"She's possessed. Probably by the same demon she summoned," I rewrapped my talisman in my hand, the other ready to grab my gun.

"You know," the demon inside of Gracie Lou said, "If I had known that it was so easy to possess someone, I'd have done it long ago."

Gracie Lou stood from the couch and Trisha tried to make me move farther back but I stood my ground. I wasn't about to let some low-level scare me off.

"You don't belong here," I gritted out.

"Well, now," the demon began, his eyes scanning me up and down and then zeroing in on my talisman. My hand tightened further around the charm and my power pulsed through it, "Neither of us belong here. Now do we, Muriel?"

My eyes widened, but I didn't back down. He wasn't the first demon to figure out what I was and who I was right from the start. They probably wouldn't be the last.

"You might be surprised that I know who you are. You've actually made quite a bit of a stir on our side of the tracks, so to speak," Gracie Lou's body moved around the office as if she were just talking about the weather.

"Mary?" Trisha's voice was uncertain, and understandably so.

Most demons didn't want to chat. They were kill-first-and-kill-kill-some-more. Whatever caused the most terror and mayhem.

"Don't worry Trisha, I've got this," I turned to where Gracie Lou had stopped at Trisha's desk, "What do you want?"

This made Gracie Lou smile and giggle. A sound that was too dark and scratchy to be coming out of such a young woman's throat.

"Why should I want anything? Maybe I just like being on this side?" she sat down in Trisha's chair and fiddled through some of the files on her desk.

I snorted, "That's hard to believe."

Gracie Lou's eyes narrowed, "It's not a laughing matter. Have you ever been to hell? Do you know what it's like there?" she stopped and smirked, "Oh, wait. I forgot. You do," Gracie Lou turned her attention to Trisha, "Did she tell you about her adventures in hell? About how they cut her up. Sawed her wings off? Oh, I heard her screams were like music to the ears."

"Stop it." The forcefulness in Trisha's voice surprised me. I'd never heard my assistant sound so angry. Even when she was freaking out on me in the car.

"What did you say to me, princess?" Gracie Lou taunted, daring her to speak up again.

"I said . . . stop it," Trisha came out from behind me, her hands on her hips, "You demons think you are something else. Like your shit doesn't stink or something. But I'm here to tell you, that you aren't anything," she stepped toward Gracie Lou, her finger pointed at the demon like a weapon, "And this woman here, you don't know anything about her."

"Trisha," I began to reach out to pull her back. I appreciated what she was trying to do but it wouldn't make a difference. It would just end up with her being hurt.

"No, Mary. Not this time," Trisha shook me off and marched over to the desk, slamming her hands down on the wooden surface, "These guys have pushed us around for the last time and I'm not going to let some hell-hole reject talk about you that way."

"What did you call me?" Gracie Lou growled out, the darkness within her rolling off of her in waves. It made Trisha take a step back. I saw Gracie Lou's hand reach out but before she could grab Trisha I shoved my assistant out of the way and looked over the barrel of my gun at the demon inside of Gracie Lou.

"Back off." I didn't know if it was the intensity of my voice or the gun pointed at Gracie Lou's head but the attacking demon suddenly became a harmless kitten once more.

"Hey, come on now. We're all friends here," Gracie Lou held her hands up and gave a nervous laugh, "There's no need for violence. Besides, you wouldn't want to hurt this innocent little girl would you?"

"Then let her go and we won't have a problem," I suggested with a shrug. The fact that I was even offering the demon a way out astounded even me. Usually, I was exorcise-first-ask-questions-later but for some reason—either Trisha's presence or the fact that I thought maybe Gracie Lou could be saved—I didn't want any more collateral damage.

Gracie Lou shook her head, "I couldn't let her go even if I wanted to."

"Explain," I gestured to her with the gun making her gulp.

"I didn't come into her uninvited. We made a deal. I teach those coworkers of hers a lesson and she gives me her soul," the demon shrugged, "The standard contract, except with a few adjustments," Gracie Lou smiled.

"Meaning, Gracie Lou didn't expect it would actually be her doing the teaching of the lesson. Or that she would be allowing you to take over her body," Trisha snapped, "You finished your work though, so why don't you just leave."

"Leave?" Gracie Lou frowned, "Why would I want to do that? The contract still stands. I get her soul when she dies and that could be a good fifty years from now."

The sheer smugness on Gracie Lou's face made my hand itch to pull the trigger, but I was trying not to kill the girl. Demons were all alike. Manipulative and self-serving. This one had taken Gracie Lou's plea for vengeance and turned it into a way to stay in the human realm.

If I knew for certain that Gracie Lou's soul would disintegrate like the rest of the humans that I'd witnessed being possessed, I'd have just let Gracie Lou and her demon go. But since the terms of the deal was until Gracie Lou dies, I had no doubt the demon would try and keep her alive as long as possible just for the fun of it.

"Fine. If I can't kill you without killing her, then I'll just have to go to a higher power," my lips quirked up as the demon's nervousness appeared on Gracie Lou's face. I kept my eyes on the girl in front of me and said to Trisha, "Call Sid. We have another deal to make."

12

LUCKY FOR ME, SID was a night owl and was still awake after three in the morning. Normally, I'd be in bed by now but after the failed robbery at the Phoenix guild and then Gracie Lou's visit, it was becoming a late night for all of us.

"What is it now?" Sid's voice was husky as if he had just woken up, or was in the middle of something particularly steamy. A part of me hoped it was the prior.

I shoved that part down and pressed my ear closer to the phone, "Did we wake you?"

"No. I mean yes," there was talking in the background and glasses clinking together. Sid let out a yawn, "Sorry. I'm still at the bar. I'm afraid I fell asleep for a moment while doing the books."

My lips ticked up on their own, "Bossman falling asleep on the job. What will the other demons say?"

"Are you teasing me, angel?" he asked with that playful tone that he used to use with me in his voice.

"No," I forced myself to frown and glared at the demon cuffed to Trisha's desk.

While Trisha had gotten her phone and called Sid, I had found a pair of handcuffs Thompson had given me as a precaution. He was tired of me incapacitating our leads before he could arrive to question them. I didn't know how he thought having handcuffs would keep me from exorcising their butts if they got too lippy. But in this case, the cuffs had proved handy.

They wouldn't keep the demon at bay for long but that's why I still had my gun out, ready to shoot if he so much as flinched. I'd tried to send Trisha home but she had refused to leave me by myself. As if *she* could help in any way. I suppose it was probably a good time to start teaching her to shoot. Then at least if she was attacked by demons she could use holy bullets to get rid of them.

"Then why are you calling me?" Sid asked again, forcing my thoughts back to the half-demon on the phone.

"I need a favor."

"Another one, angel?" Sid sighed heavily. "Haven't you gotten yourself into enough trouble already? I don't want to be the reason you end up back in hell."

"I didn't know you cared about me that much," I retorted.

Gracie Lou laughed. A cackle that belonged in a horror movie, and not in my waiting area.

"What's so funny?" I asked moving my mouth away from the phone.

"Here I am, cuffed to your chair and you are chit-chatting with your lover," she began to laugh hysterically banging her hand against the surface of the desk.

"Mary?" Sid said in my ear, "What's going on? Who was that?"

Ignoring his questions, I pointed the gun back at Gracie Lou, "Shut your mouth before I give you another one."

"Oh, but you wouldn't want to hurt your precious girl, now would you?" Gracie Lou pouted and then gave me an evil smile.

"No, but that doesn't mean I won't still hurt you," I aimed the gun lower until it was pointed at the demon's arm, "Test me and I'll show you what a holy bullet feels like."

This made her shut up quickly and I turned my attention back to Sid who was still talking in my ear, "As you can hear, I have kind of a demon problem on my hands."

Sid sighed, "When do you not? Seriously, I think you purposely go looking for trouble angel."

That wasn't even close to true. Okay, so maybe it was a little true. When you are searching for your wings and trying to get revenge on your jailers it was a little hard not to get sucked into demon politics. And now that I was trying to find Ramiel things just kept getting more and more complicated. Gracie Lou though was another story altogether.

"For your information, this one happens to be a client. Or was supposed to be a client until I told her I wouldn't raise a demon to attack some coworkers who were bullying her."

"People come to you for that?" I could hear the disbelief in his voice and I didn't blame him.

Before Gracie Lou, I didn't even know people thought of demon attacks as a thing to do as revenge. Especially not humans. I would have expected her to do something more human, like report it to her boss or trash their car. Not summon a demon from hell to terrorize them. Where she'd even gotten the idea from I didn't know. I could only blame television.

The few times I had even bothered to watch any of what humans called entertainment, I had felt weirdly violated. The comedies were alright. There were heartfelt stories that I could understand people wanting to watch, but then there were shows and movies that were all about lying and cheating. Even murder. Shows purposely used to scare the crap out of their audience.

One night after Trisha had learned I was an angel, she made me watch *The Exorcist*. She'd thought I would get a kick out of it. All it had done was make me think humans had weird minds and didn't know what real horror was. But I could see how it would give plenty of people ideas. Ideas like the one Gracie Lou had when she'd come to me in the first place.

"Apparently, so," I replied after a moment, "The longer I stay on earth the more I see how truly warped these humans are. Why God loves them so much is beyond me."

"And yet you stay with them," Sid pointed out, "And spend all your time with them."

"Not like I have much of a choice," I snapped, "I can't get back to heaven without my wings, and the only other angel I know that is on earth is Ramiel. Hell, I'd settle for a fallen angel right now. Just to try to figure another way out."

"Be careful what you wish for, angel," Sid muttered almost too low for me to hear. Then in his normal voice, he said, "So what do you want me to do? Talk this girl out of it?"

"No, it's too late for that," I turned my attention back to the demon who was intently watching Trisha. Trisha glared at it while she snapped a photo on her cell phone. Letting out an aggravated sigh, I marched over to Trisha and snatched her phone from her.

"This isn't something you should be taking photos of. We are in a real crisis here. You should be —"

"Mary, watch out!" Trisha yelled out as I was hit from behind. Thrown to the ground, my phone skidded across the room. I scrambled to my feet and spun around.

While I had been paying attention to Trisha I'd had turned my back on the demon who had broken free of his binds. She sat on top of Trisha, Gracie Lou's small hands wrapped around my assistant's neck, squeezing hard. Trisha kicked out and clawed at the fingers at her throat with her hands. But there was no way she was going to break the demon's hold. Gracie Lou might have been a small girl but possessed like she was, her strength would have tripled.

I pointed the gun at Gracie Lou, "Let her go."

She hissed at me, Gracie Lou's eyes filming over with white, and an animal-like snarl twisted her features.

"Do it. Or I will shoot you," I warned once more, but the demon inside just laughed. I aimed for Gracie Lou's shoulder and didn't even think about it when I squeezed the trigger. The bullet rang true and the Gracie Lou demon let out a howl and let go of Trisha.

With the gun still pointed at the demon, I knelt down and pulled Trisha away from her. Trisha gulped in air as she rubbed her throat and coughed. I held her close to me, my eyes never leaving the girl, who was nursing her wound as she leaned against on the opposite wall.

"Are you alright?"

"Just peachy," Trisha croaked out. It made me want to shoot the demon again, Gracie Lou be damned.

"Good. Get the phone. I think it went over there by my door somewhere," I gestured across the room with my head.

"You shot me, you bitch!" the demon screamed and jumped up to attack me, but I fired again, this time at the other arm. The demon inside of Gracie Lou twitched causing the girl's whole body to convulse.

"Sit the down or I'll shoot you again," I snapped.

"You'll kill her," the demon taunted, holding her new wound even though I was pretty sure it had already stopped bleeding. Demons healed fast even when possessing another, holy bullets or not.

"Oh, stop your whining. It's not a fatal injury," I waved the gun in her direction and then glanced briefly at Trisha who had retrieved my phone.

I could hear Sid yelling into the phone even before it was up to my ear.

"What the hell is going on there? Mary? Answer me. Are you alright?" the panic in his voice made something in my heart squeeze tight.

"Calm down, I'm fine," I said into the phone while watching the Gracie Lou demon coddle his wounds.

I should have shot her in the head and gotten it over with. A few years ago, I would have without a second thought. Now though—maybe it was the part of me that was becoming more human—the thought of killing her even though she deserved it, made me sick.

"Wait there. I'm coming over," Sid commanded. There was some shuffling and then a car door slammed. An engine roared to life—no doubt Sid's big truck.

"Isn't your license still suspended? You shouldn't be driving," I commented. "Besides, I just need you to get daddy dearest to make this demon break its contract, or say the contract is complete, so he will let this poor girl's body go. There's no need for you to come down here."

"Even more reason for me to come. I'm not letting you make another deal with my father without me there. You are already in too deep as it is." I could hear the disapproval in his voice. Apparently, even though he was half demon he either didn't approve of making deals—or was it just the one I made with his father?

"I'm a big girl. I can take care of myself. Besides, why can't I do for your father what you couldn't?" Trisha tugged at my arm and I told Sid to hold on. "What is it?"

"I think I'm going to call it a night. If you don't mind," she rubbed her throat once more where purple and blue marks were

155

beginning to form, "I think I've had enough excitement for one night."

"Oh, Trish. Of course, I should have sent you home the moment we got here," I place a hand on her arm, "Don't worry about me. I've got this and Sid's on his way so I won't be alone."

"Are you going to make another deal with Asmodeus?" Trisha asked, her eyes narrowing, "Don't you think we are in a bit too deep as it is?" her eyes darted to Gracie Lou and back to me, "Maybe we should just let the demon have her. Or just put her out of her misery. It has to be better than whatever that monster will ask of you in return."

"Patricia!" I cried out, "I'm surprised at you. You'd let an innocent human suffer?"

"To keep you safe? After what she did?" she shot Gracie Lou a look of disgust, "Yes. A hundred percent yes."

I shook my head in sadness. "I appreciate your worry but there's hardly much Asmodeus can do to me that hasn't already been done. Besides," I gave her a small smile, "If he asks for too much I'll say no and just put her out of her misery."

"If you're sure. But I don't want you to end up giving your life for someone who doesn't deserve it."

I laughed and gave Trisha a little push toward the door, "I'm an angel Trisha, not a saint. I'm hardly selfless."

After one more worrying look from Trisha, she was gone and I was alone with my possessed would-be client. And Sid, who was probably still on the phone.

"Sid? Are you still there?" I asked, but he didn't answer. I looked at the screen of the phone; he'd hung up. Shrugging, I put my phone in my back pocket and turned my attention back to my guest.

My gaze locked onto Gracie Lou who had stopped moaning over her wounds. I had four more bullets in the magazine. I hoped I wouldn't have to shoot her again but if it came down to it I'd do exactly what I'd told Trisha. Put the poor thing out of her misery. There'd be no future for the girl as long as that demon lived inside of her.

"Good idea, sending your girl away. We wouldn't want her to get hurt," Gracie Lou snickered and I itched to shoot her again.

Restraining myself, I pulled Trisha's chair out from behind her desk and sat on it in front of the demon. "You guys don't really know when to shut up, do you? You just keep pushing and pushing. One of these days, you demon scum are going to push me too far and I'll just kill you all."

"And for an angel, you aren't very holy," Gracie Lou shot back. "Aren't you supposed to be some perfect portrayal of all things good and nice." The girl's lips twisted as the demon sneered at the word.

I smirked at her description. "Maybe once upon a time, I was. I honestly can't remember anymore. Your kind changed that," I pointed at her, "Now, I can see what I had been so blind to before. The world is full of hate and most of the humans aren't worth saving. Even worse, are you demons. Not a good one among you," I spat, "Nothing but a bunch of bottom feeders not worthy to even show your faces to the outside world. Demon, half-demon, what does it matter? You all belong in hell and I'm going to do my best to make sure you stay there."

The demon didn't react the way I'd expected. In fact, she only smiled at me as if she had a secret. Then someone cleared their throat and I jumped from my seat.

Spinning around, there was Sidney standing in my front door.

"Well, it's nice to know where I rate in your mind, angel."

13

SEEING THE HURT ON Sid's face shouldn't have affected me. I had just claimed I thought all of his kind should be in hell. That I didn't care for any of them. But if that was true, why did my throat feel like I had something stuck in it? And why did my chest hurt?

"Sid," I breathed out. "What are you doing here?"

Dressed in his usual dark jeans and tight-fitted shirt, there was no doubt whose son he was. If there was anything redeeming about Asmodeus, the demon lord knew how to make a good looking child. Sid tucked his hands in his pockets and moved across the room. "Saving you as usual." The bitterness in his voice made me wince.

"I told you not to come. I have it under control," I gestured to Gracie Lou who was still curled up against the wall, but the look of delight on her face was just asking to be shot.

"Yes," the demon hissed and laughed, "Muriel and I were having just the nicest time. We don't need you, half-breed."

Sid brushed passed me, no longer paying me any mind, his gaze firmly set on the demon before us. He knelt beside Gracie Lou and turned his head this way and that as if looking for something. Gracie Lou didn't attack him. Instead she just watched Sid in return, as if they were sizing each other up.

After a moment, Sid stood. He walked over to me and stopped, "Just kill her. You're better off killing her than wasting your time with my father."

I ground my teeth together. "I thought you of all people would want me to save her. Wasn't it you who said that I needed to embrace my humanity? Well, this is my chance."

Sid shook his head, his brown hair falling over his eyes. "Not this one, angel. There's a time and place for self-sacrifice

161

and this isn't one of them. That girl was already doomed. Even if my father makes him break the contract, it won't save her soul. She made the deal and now she has to live with the consequences. All you can do is lessen her suffering now."

My hand tightened on my gun and then flipped the safety on and holstered it. Crossing my arms over my chest, I glared at him. "No."

"No?" Sid raised a brow at me, "What do you mean no?"

"No, I'm not going to do that. I made a promise to myself to lower the number of casualties I create because of my vendetta. I won't break that promise. Not when I could save her."

"But you can't," Sid tried to grab my shoulders but I shoved him away and turned my back to him. He let out an aggravated sigh, "Why are you being so stubborn about this?"

"I'm not being stubborn," I snapped, spinning back around, "I'm trying to do what is right and you are being an ass."

The demon laughed and Gracie Lou's voice echoed around the room. Sid and I both turned our heads to her and yelled, "Shut up."

Then, Sid shifted his attention to my face. "I'm being an ass? he stepped toward me, his nostrils flaring. "I'm just trying to help you. That's all I've ever tried to do."

"Well, stop. I don't need or want your help," I shoved my finger at his chest.

"But you will take my father's?" Sid scoffed.

"At least, he can get things done," I retorted, "If you're going to be a demon, at least be one with power."

It was a cheap shot, I knew, but I had decided to save Gracie Lou and I'd be damned if anyone tried to make me decide otherwise. I wouldn't have called him had I known how to get in contact with Asmodeus myself. Not that I wanted to ask the demon lord for any more help than he had already promised to provide. That was *if* he came through on his part. For all I knew he might be jerking me around. Lower demons might have to follow through on their deals, but when you were one of the big bads, the rules were bendable.

"Fine," Sid growled, "you want to see power? I'll show you power," he grabbed the rosary wrapped around his wrist and pulled it off with such force that the beads scattered to the ground.

My mouth dropped open and I half-stepped toward him to stop him but it was too late. The lights flickered and the room filled with a thickness that I could only describe as pure evil. It made my skin crawl and even the Gracie Lou recoiled from it. Without thinking, I pulled my gun from its holster, the end of it pointed at my former friend.

To an outsider, it would look like Sid was about to have a panic attack, but to someone who knew what to look for it would be obvious that something else more malignant was happening. His body pulsated, causing my vision to wobble as I tried to focus on him. Getting a headache from looking at him, I dropped the veil so that I could see all of him and what I saw made my insides scream.

Pure darkness swirled around inside of Sid, so powerful that it leaked over the edges of his body and filled the room. None of what used to be Sid even existed anymore. As I closed the veil back, not able to stand to look at what had once been my friend, a chilling grin spread across his face.

"Is this what you wanted, Muriel? Am I demon enough for you?" he purred and the sound rumbled along my skin and settled inside me, making me ache in places that had no business waking up.

"What the hell did you do?" Gracie Lou yelled from his place against the wall, "You didn't tell me that this guy was *his* son. You've doomed us both."

Glaring at the cowardly demon, I tightened my grip on my Glock and turned my attention back to the creature Sid had become. He still looked like Sid, but he also didn't. The tattoos decorating his arms stood out more and the gold in his eyes—usually a green-and-gold mixture— had bled over to be completely golden. The way he was looking at me though was the worst of it. As if he wanted to find out what I tasted like and I knew if I let him near me, I wouldn't be able to stop it from happening.

"Fine, you've proved your point," I said my voice a bit more breathless than I intended it to be, "Now reel it back."

"Too late for that. You wanted me this way and now you've got me," Sid laughed and moved toward me, each step forcing me to take a step back in response. We did this for a few moments; he'd take a step and then I would until my back ended up against the wall and I had nowhere else to go. But that didn't stop Sid. He kept coming until the barrel of my gun was pressed into his chest.

"Back off, I mean it." Even to me, my voice sounded helpless and not at all convincing. I gulped as he glanced down at my gun and simply pushed it to the side. The lack of resistance on my part didn't bode well for any of us.

"Now, you don't really think you are going to shoot me, do you?" he tut-tutted at me before he caged me between his arms against the wall. Sid moved in until his mouth was against my ear. His breath hot against it as he said, "Admit it, angel, you like me this way. You want me to be some horrible monster that you can just kill and forget about. That way you can

166

forget everything about how I make you feel."

His words made my body clench and soften beneath him and I let out a whimper. I didn't know if it was a protest or an encouragement. My body wasn't my own anymore, so overwhelmed by the power he had over me.

"If you guys are going to fuck, I am so out of here," my eyes darted from Sid to Gracie Lou who got up from the ground and quickly crossed the room. Before he could get to the threshold though, Sid's hand shot out and slammed the door shut on the other side of the room.

"Don't leave just yet," Sid smirked his words for the demon within Gracie Lou but his eyes all on me, "Mary wants to break your deal and since Mary always gets what she wants, you're not going anywhere."

Gracie Lou froze in place at his words. Slowly turning on her heel, she shook her head, her uncertainty clear on her face, "You don't have that kind of authority. You can't make me do anything."

"Can't I?" he countered and then closed his hand in a tight fist causing the demon to fall to the ground. She clutched her head and screamed a low agonizing sound, one that I knew all too well. I knew what it felt like to scream myself raw, hoping and praying that the pain would stop.

As usual, thinking about my past caused my scars to itch and it was enough to break whatever spell Sid had on me. Body still yearning, I shoved Sid in the chest.

"That's enough. I want to save her, not kill her," I pointed the gun back at Sid and thankfully my hand didn't waver this time.

"I'm not hurting her, just the demon inside. Isn't that right, underling?" Sid asked the demon as its screams became so loud I could hardly think.

"How do I know that? For all I know, you could be killing her right this second," I shot back as Gracie Lou's screams turned to racking sobs.

"But why should you care?" he barked. "You don't have any connection to these creatures. They are weak useless selfish beings. Someone of your stature shouldn't bother with such trivial matters," his eyes roamed up and down my form. My hand tightening on my gun until it bit into my palm as I pushed back the feeling that came from his gaze.

"I suppose you think the same way about Trisha too, then? Too bad you just missed her. She could have been your next victim," I snapped, hoping by mentioning my assistant he might come back to his senses.

"Maybe I'll pay a visit to her next," he gave me a vicious grin before turning back to Gracie Lou.

My patience gone, I took the few steps I needed to be right next to him and pressed the barrel of my gun against his head. "Stop. I won't ask you again and this time, I will shoot you."

Sid paused and Gracie Lou stopped screaming. There was a fraction of a moment where I thought I had finally gotten through to him before he threw his arm out, hitting me in the chest. I flew across the room, my back slamming against the same wall Gracie Lou had recently been cowering against.

Breath knocked out of me, I wasn't fast enough to stop Sid as he landed before me. He wrapped one hand around my neck and pulled me up until my feet dangled in the air. Clawing at his hand, I gasped for breath while his grip tightened around my throat.

"Do not think that just because the human side of me loves you that I will not kill you," Sid ground out his fingers digging into my flesh.

"Sid," I croaked out, "Sidney, stop." If he didn't let me go I was going to have to hurt him. And not the I'll-shoot-you kind of hurt or the I'd exorcise-your-ass kind of hurt. No, the kind that made me weak for days afterward and ended with Sidney Magnus no longer existing.

If Sid registered my words he didn't show it. His hand kept squeezing and I was beginning to see spots. Just as I was about to draw on my reservoir of holy powers—my trump card if things ever got really bad—a familiar voice asked, "Now, what do we have here?"

Sid and Gracie Lou stopped in place at the sound of the demon lord's voice but I didn't share their fear. I kicked my foot out, hitting Sid between the legs and fell to the ground as he let go of me to clutch at his injured bits.

Gasping for breath, I grabbed my aching throat. I'd never been more happy to see the demon lord in my life. If he wasn't a demon I could have kissed him right then. Instead, I threw my hands up in the air and said, "Finally! Took you long enough."

14

"MURIEL, YOU HAVE BEEN a naughty naughty angel." Asmodeus clicked his tongue as he took in the scene around him.

With Sid's attention on his father, I slowly moved from the floor and as far from Sid as I could get. Didn't want to experience that again.

Asmodeus glanced at his son and then at Gracie Lou sprawled on the floor. Making a humming in the back of his throat, he moved from the middle of the room over to where I was crouched. Offering me a hand, he said, "You are lucky I got here in time. One more minute and I'm afraid I wouldn't have been able to help you."

I eyed his hand for a moment and then sighed and took it. He was saving my butt,

172

so I couldn't afford to be rude. Who knew what he would ask from me in return?

"How did you even know to come?" I cocked a brow at him as he helped me to my feet.

"Our dear Sidney contacted me on his way over." He smiled and gestured to his son who was waiting like a good child—or rather a snake biding his time. "I, unfortunately, was preoccupied and couldn't get here right away. But it looks like all's well that ends well."

He turned to leave but I reached out and grabbed his arm before he could disappear on me. "Wait."

Asmodeus paused and turned to me with an expectant expression. "Yes?"

"Aren't you going to take care of them?" I waved a hand at the two demons still frozen in the middle of my waiting area. I wished I had that kind of presence to stop my enemies in their tracks. Alas, even on a good day I was lucky to get them to take my threats seriously.

"Take care of them? How so?" His head angled to the side, making him look more boyish in his Hollywood-star body. He was going to make me work for this. Typical demon.

I gritted my teeth and said, "I want Gracie Lou freed. It's not right that the demon inside of her can just latch on until she dies. She didn't agree to that."

"Ah, but didn't she?" Asmodeus gave a cruel grin. "She summoned the demon. It is her responsibility to specify the terms of her arrangement. If not," he held his hands up and shrugged, "It is for her to deal with the consequences."

"But that's not fair!" I snapped and wanted to stomp my foot like a petulant child.

"Life isn't fair. You should know." He looked me over as if he could see something I couldn't. "Did you think your God would abandon you when you came after your precious friend?"

I didn't answer him, and my lips pressing hard together as I frowned. I knew he was right. That life wasn't fair. Even for an angel. Especially for an angel like me.

When I had chased after Ramiel that day, so long ago, I'd never expected to be captured. Even worse, I'd never considered

174

the possibility that nobody would anyone come after me. Those first few weeks I'd prayed with all my might for God to come save me. That someone, anyone, would come but they never did. I had learned then I was on my own and would always be on my own. Even if I did eventually get back to heaven. Sometimes I wondered if it was even worth it anymore.

"How about this?" Asmodeus said, walking around to where Gracie Lou sat on the floor. She reminded me of an abused child. Sitting there waiting to be told what to do, but not wanting to do anything in case their parent would lash out at them.

"I'll help you with this and then you would..." he trailed off, tapping his chin and then he grinned. "Owe me one."

"No." I didn't even hesitate.

"No? I thought you wanted to help this poor girl who had gotten in over her head." He reached down and grabbed Gracie Lou's curls, yanking her to her feet making the demon inside whimper, "Or I could do us all a favor and get rid of her now. Would that be better?"

"No," I yelled taking a step forward. My hands clenched into tight fists until my nails bit into my palms, "Fine. We can make a deal. Just..." I sighed and gestured to Gracie Lou, "...help her, okay?"

The smile that curled up his face was nothing if not wicked and I wondered what the hell I had done, and if this girl was really worth it.

"Very well," Asmodeus nodded once and then turned back to the girl at his feet, "Stand."

The tone in his voice had turned from a nice pleasant sound to a commanding one that made the air in the room thicken. A sound even worse than when Sid had first let his demon side free. It made Gracie Lou scramble to her feet, a visible tremor going through her body.

Asmodeus stared at the girl for a moment, not saying anything. And then hissed, "My'ac. Come forth."

Gracie Lou's body convulsed and her eyes rolled up into the back of her head. Her mouth opened wide and blackness spewed out of her. Unlike when I usually exorcised demons, this one didn't

176

immediately go back to hell. Instead, he sat before Asmodeus's feet.

"Master," the demon My'ac hissed. I'd never heard a demon speak out of a physical form. I had only ever met demons in their true form, or when they were possessing a human. I didn't even think it was possible for them to speak this way. Shows what I know.

"Your contract with the human is nullified," Asmodeus commanded.

"But, Master she—" My'ac tried to argue, but Asmodeus's hand shot out and grabbed a hold of the smoke-like body, cutting the demon's words off. It went against all logic that he was able to touch the intangible demon, but he was a demon lord. Who was I to question what he was and wasn't able to do. All the more reason why I shouldn't give him Michael's blade.

"Do not argue with me," Asmodeus growled, "you will do as you are told. The contract is over. Go back to the hole you crawled out of." Asmodeus threw the demon away from him where it fell to the ground. My'ac's form shuddered for a moment. If he showed any sign of agreement I couldn't tell because the next thing I know he'd disappeared into the floor and was gone.

I rushed to Gracie Lou's side and pressed my fingers to the side of her neck. She still had a pulse. Her chest moved up and down slowly and I let out a breath. She was alive, but unconscious.

"She'll wake up after a few hours. You know how exhausting possession can be on these frail human bodies."

I glared at the demon lord and picked Gracie Lou up in my arms. Crossing the room, I laid her on my lumpy couch before spinning on my heel to point at him.

"You fixed her, now fix him." I jerked my head toward Sid. Who was still waiting like a patient lap dog, for his father's command.

"What? Why would I want to do that?" he chuckled and went over to Sid. Clapping him on the shoulders, he then patted the side of Sid's face. "He's so much more obedient when he isn't trying to pretend he's human."

Sid's jaw tightened and I could see a flicker of something. Maybe defiance? Anger? Whatever it was it was gone before

Asmodeus could register it. Maybe things weren't all they appeared.

"Because he's not himself. He tried to kill me," I argued, my hands on my hips.

Asmodeus shrugged a shoulder and half turned to me. "What can I say? Boys will be boys. You shouldn't have egged him on."

"Yeah, right," I scoffed, the urge to spit on him almost too much to resist, "I did no such thing, and Sid wouldn't be happy to know what he'd done."

"How do you know?" Asmodeus asked and then turned his attention to Sid. "Are you happy Sidney? Doesn't it feel so much better to be your true self? To be free?"

Sid glanced at me for a moment and then smiled at his father, "Never felt better."

"See?" the demon lord slapped Sid on the back and laughed. "Why would I want to ruin such a perfect son?"

"Because he almost killed me," I pointed out again.

"You're one of the big and mighty archangels. Are you telling me you can't handle on little wittle half demon?" He squeezed his thumb and forefinger together until there was only about an inch between them.

I shot a look at Sid before crossing my arms over my chest, "I can handle myself, but I don't think you will be very happy when I have to put a bullet in your son's brain. Or worse." When Asmodeus blanched, I smirked.

Checkmate.

"Why should I care?" he tried to be flippant about it but I knew his game. He'd already shown his cards, and now I had him by the balls—as Trisha would say.

"Well now, let's think about this for a moment," I tapped the side of my face as my other hand fingered my gun, "I could kill your son, or he could kill me. Either way, you lose."

"How do you figure that?"

"You still need me," I tilted my head to the side and raised an brow, "or did you find someone else to steal Michael's blade for you?"

Asmodeus' face reddened. If we were in one of those cartoons Trisha liked to watch, I'd imagine he'd have steam coming out of his ears. I would have laughed had the situation been more appropriate. I think if I had laughed then, Asmodeus would have said screw the blade, and would have killed me anyways.

"Very well," Asmodeus adjusted the cuffs of his shirt and then pulled on his collar, "You have won this round, Muriel." He said my name as if it tasted like garbage in his mouth. "But do not get complacent. I could still kill you," and then he grinned, "or better yet, I could kill your little friend."

"Have you found him?" I tried to keep the eagerness out of my voice but from the look on Asmodeus's face, I had failed.

"Not yet, but when I do, I'll make sure to let him know you sent me." His eyes had a twinkle in them that promised pain. Pain that he would inflict on Ramiel for my backtalk. Backing out of the deal now seemed better and better. If only I could be sure he wouldn't go after Ramiel just to spite me.

"As for your part," Asmodeus took a step toward me and I forced myself to stay in place, "Have you acquired what I have asked?" his eyes searched over me and then he frowned, "I do not feel it here."

"There were complications," I stated crossing my arms over my chest, "You didn't tell me it was a hunter's guild I was breaking into."

"Oh?" his brows shot up, "Was it? I had no idea." The smile on his face said otherwise.

"I could have gotten killed," I growled. More importantly, Trisha could have gotten hurt again.

Asmodeus held his hands out, "Yet here you are. Alive and unharmed, save for my son's little present," he gestured to my throbbing neck and I was sure I'd have a necklace of bruises later.

"That's beside the point," I clenched my jaw, restraining myself from attacking him just because he was being a pain, "I would have been more prepared had I known. I could actually have been able to acquire the blade."

"Well, now you know. And you can do better next time," he gave me a condescending smile and then turned away from me, "I'll be in touch. And Muriel?"

"What?"

"Don't take too long. Angels are such delicate creatures. You never know when one might break."

I took a step toward him as he laughed, about ready to show him how delicate a creature I really was when Sid's hand shot out and grabbed my arm. Glaring up at him, I realized the person looking back at me was actually Sid and not his demon alter ego.

My gaze went back to where Asmodeus had been, but the demon lord was already gone. Damn demons.

Turning back to Sid, I looked him over, searching for any sign of his other self. But somehow, during our exchange, Asmodeus had fixed him. I looked to the floor of my office and saw the beads of his rosary still scattered there. My eyes jerked back to Sid and my mouth opened to ask how, but before I could get the words out Sid spoke.

"My father has a way with demons. Raising them up," he tucked his hand in his pockets and kicked the floor slightly, "And pushing them down."

"I figured as much," I shifted so that I could slip from Sid's grip. He let me go and waited, as if not sure what to do with himself. I wasn't sure either. I had already been pissed at him before, but now I really should hate him. For some reason I didn't.

"So that's your demon side," I said, then let out a nervous chuckle, "he needs to work on his manners."

Sid's lips ticked up at the edges, "Yeah, he's a real asshole."

After an awkward moment, we both burst out laughing. We were pretending everything was alright when it really wasn't, but what else could we do? Arguing and yelling about it wouldn't solve anything, and I had enough enemies. I was tired of fighting.

I bent at the waist as I tried to catch my breath, my hand reaching out to hold onto Sid's bicep so I wouldn't topple over. His arm flexed underneath my fingers and my laughter caught in my throat.

Our eyes met and I licked my lips. His gaze darted down to watch the movement and I felt that special tickle in my lower region. Clearing my throat, I dropped my hand from his arm and backed up until I was next to Gracie Lou.

"I should really make sure she's okay," I looked down at the sleeping girl, "Maybe call the cops."

"Cops?" Sid asked coming up next to me. I forced myself not to look at him, not sure I'd be able to keep myself from touching him again. He might have been onto something when he'd said he'd never made me attracted to him. Just standing there made my skin ache to be near him.

"Yeah, the demon might be gone but it still killed several people before it left," I sighed, "She might not know it but even though she's not possessed anymore, she'll have to answer for those deaths."

"Won't she be mad?"

I shook my head, "No, I think she will want to pay for what she's done. Otherwise, it'll feel like the demon is still here. Her life would be haunted by what she did. Still will, even if she goes to jail."

"That sucks. Guess you can't save everyone," Sid commented and I nodded.

"Yeah, it seems like it."

15

AFTER I SENT SID on his way, I called up Thompson. I kept several details out of what happened, like Asmodeus being back and Sid going full demon on me, giving the detective only the gist of it.

"And she's with you now?" Thompson asked, "Is she secure?"

"Thompson," I sighed and rubbed my eyes. It had been a long night and I wanted nothing more than to curl up in my bed and sleep for a week, "Gracie Lou is not going to hurt anyone and for that matter, she's probably too traumatized by what happened to even function if she wakes up."

"What do you mean if?"

Moving to sit down on the chair by the desk, I stared at Gracie Lou's unconscious form. "Most humans don't survive being possessed. The demons eat away at their souls until they don't exist anymore. Those who do..."

"Yeah?" Thompson urged me on.

I sighed again. "Those who do, aren't themselves anymore. They spook easily. Are irritable at best, and more often than not they end up in mental institutions or worse, finishing what the demon started."

"So, you're saying she's unstable? Or will be," Thompson commented as if he were writing it all down, which knowing him he probably was, "So, what is your suggestion?"

I glanced at Gracie Lou and frowned, "It really depends on how she is when she wakes up. She didn't mean to kill anyone. Hell, she just wanted to make them stop teasing her. It was just a prank gone wrong."

"Tell that to the parents of her coworkers," Thompson bit out, "Do you know where she killed them at?"

"No," I shook my head even though he couldn't see it, "But I'm sure someone will find them soon. Demons aren't known for being discreet."

187

"Alright," he said, "I'll send someone over to collect her and have someone get a list of her coworkers. Do you know where she worked?"

I sighed, getting a little aggravated, "No, she didn't tell me anything other than her name and what she wanted me to do. But I'm sure you can figure it out."

Thompson gave a short laugh, "Like a needle in a haystack, but we'll figure it out. Thanks, Wiles."

"No problem," I hung up the phone and waited at Trisha's desk for the officers to show up. I didn't have long to wait. There was a knock on my door not more than twenty minutes later. Two officers, one male and one female, entered.

"She's over here," I gestured to Gracie Lou who was lying on the couch.

"You didn't restrain her?" the male accused with a frown.

I gave him an impatient look. "No, she's passed out and probably will be for a while. Did you call an ambulance?"

"No," the woman answered this time, "We were just told to go pick up a murder suspect. We didn't expect..." She glanced at the innocently sleeping form of Gracie Lou.

I didn't blame them. At first glance, I hadn't imagined she would kill a bunch of people either. And she hadn't. The demon who'd possessed her had, but the cops didn't know that. As far as they were concerned Gracie Lou was a crazy murderess.

"Just be careful with her and have Thompson call me when she wakes up," I glanced down at Gracie Lou once more, "And don't put her near anything sharp."

"You think she'll kill again?" the female officer asked, worry on her face.

"Only herself."

"Got it," the male officer moved over to the couch and slid his arms under Gracie Lou, lifting her with ease, "She's on suicide watch, then." He nodded at me before heading for the door.

"You have a good night, ma'am," the female cop nodded as well and then followed her partner out of my office. I closed and locked the door behind them, and then sagged against it.

Finally.

* * *

I DIDN'T REMEMBER GOING to bed. I just remembered waking up to a pounding sound from the other room.

I groaned and rolled over in bed, my clothes pulling tight at my body. I had fallen asleep in my clothes, which meant I hadn't taken a shower last night. The icky stink of demon covered me, making my body heavy and my stomach sick.

I lay there for a moment, trying to convince myself that the pounding I had heard was in my dreams and not in real life. Sadly though, reality crashed down on me when the unwanted sound became real once more.

Dragging myself from the bed, I glanced at my clock. Nine a.m. Meaning I'd had less than a three hours of sleep and my mood even worse.

I gritted my teeth and grabbed my gun from its holster by the bed. At least, I'd remembered to take that off before I'd passed out. No need to shoot myself in the middle of the night.

I trudged out of my office-slash-bedroom and into the waiting area. Trisha hadn't arrived yet, which I thought was strange until I remembered I gave her the day off after almost she'd almost died again last night.

Frowning at the area, I made a note to get Madame Serena to perform a cleansing. The whole office reeked of demon. Most people wouldn't notice. They would just feel a bit uncomfortable. But to someone like me, or anyone even a bit psychic, the room would make you physically ill. I was lucky to keep the bile from rising as I yanked the front door open.

Before I could even register who was standing in front of me a hand popped out of nowhere and slapped me on the side of the face. My cheek stung and I shook my head.

"What the hell is wrong with you?" a familiar voice screeched at me.

My eyes came back into focus as I took in the woman before me. Kelly Larsen, Trisha's mother, stood before me. The complete opposite of my assistant, she stood as poised and graceful as ever.

Bleached-blonde hair pulled back in a tight bun, perfectly applied make that wasn't too obvious and accented her features. Blue-green eyes narrowed at me, the disgust and anger there not hard to distinguish.

The rest of the woman was a put together as her upper extremities. She wore a pale pink suit with sensible shoes. A matching bag hung on her shoulder and her nails were painted a pretty shade of coral.

"Mrs. Larsen, good to see you again," I put on a fake smile and forced myself not to comment on her attack on me. I'd learned the best way to deal with her was get it over with as quickly as possible.

I moved away from the door and into the office, not caring if she followed me. Sure enough, though, she stomped through the door and shoved a finger me.

"Don't give me that crap," she snapped, "I let my daughter work for you because we wanted her to stay out of trouble. After that hacking incident, we thought she would be safe here. A desk job answering phones," Kelly gestured around the room, blatant disgust on her face. I tried not to take it personally. My office wasn't that great to begin with, and with demon sludge all over, it probably didn't add to its appeal.

"And I appreciate Trisha's work," I replied, "She does a great job and has been a model employee."

"Good. Then you can give Patricia a good reference because my daughter will not be working here any longer. I forbid it," Kelly crossed her arms over her chest and stared me down. Her expression might have scared some of the mother's in the PTA but I faced down demons every day. All it did was make me annoyed.

"Last time I checked Trisha was eighteen and can work where she wants," I countered. A part of me wondered if Trisha put her mother up to this. That she was too scared of what I might do to come herself, but I brushed it off. Trisha wasn't that kind of girl. She'd always been a ball-buster and it had only gotten worse since my true lineage had been revealed. No, Kelly Larsen was here all on her own.

"But she still lives under my house and as long as that continues she will not be working for someone like you," she spat the word as if I was something on the bottom of her shoe to scrap off on the sidewalk.

"Someone like me?" I drew out, my anger beginning to swell, "And what exactly am I, Mrs. Larsen?"

"A parasite," she growled stepping closer until we were toe-to-toe, her nose almost brushing against mine, "A waste-of-space piece of trash who should know better than to drag a good girl like Patricia down with her."

Honestly, I could disagree with her. Trisha was a good kid, even if she had a penchant for getting into trouble. I know my goal wasn't something I should drag an innocent into. Revenge never was pretty. But even if I tried to send her away, I knew she'd come back, probably yelling up a storm about me treating her like a child. The same way her mother was doing now, though she was probably coming here without Trisha's permission.

Kelly didn't know that her description of me was pretty far off though. I couldn't be further from a parasite. Not like the demons I hunted. But she didn't need to know that. Nor did she need to know what

I was. All she needed to know was that her daughter would be safe in my care. And while last night I might have backslid a bit I was determined—more now than ever—to keep her out of it.

"You're right," I said after a moment causing Kelly's eyes to widen. I stepped back from her and shrugged. "I'm probably not a great person for your daughter to hang around but..." I narrowed my eyes on the woman before me, an unyielding tone in my voice, "that is for Trisha to decide, not you. As far as I'm concerned she will always be welcome here. And if she wants to leave," I waved a hand to the side, "Fine. I'll let her go without argument and would be more than happy to give her a glowing recommendation. But," I snapped the word, "Until that time, I will have to ask you to leave."

Kelly's mouth fell open and then after a moment, her face scrunched up. "How dare you?" she spat, looking me up and down, "How dare you talk to me about what is best for Trisha when you sent her home last night with bruises on her neck. Similar to those on your own," her eyes darted to my neck and I almost reached up to touch them. But I resisted.

"What kind of person, what kind of place is this that you would let not only yourself, but your employee get hurt?" she asked. But before I could answer she grabbed her phone out of her purse, "I should call the police on you. Tell them exactly what kind of place you are running here."

That made me laugh, which was the wrong thing to do. Kelly glared at me and started dialing the phone. I watched her with a smile on my face.

"Hello," Kelly said into the phone, her eyes narrowed on me, "I'd like to report a crime." The person on the other line said something and then Kelly went on, "I want to report Wiles Investigation for unfit work conditions," The person on the other line said something again making Kelly frown, "Yes, that Mary Wiles. Yes, I'll hold for the Sergeant," she shooting me a grin as if she had won something. But if I was a betting woman, and I wasn't, she was about to eat her words.

"Yes, hello. Sergeant Thompson, is it? I'm told you can help me with a problem."

I could hear Thompson's gruff voice from the phone and forced myself not to laugh. "What's the problem? The problem is this woman — Mary Wiles. She has gotten my daughter hurt while working for her. Just last night she came home with bruises all over neck!"

Thompson must have said something she didn't like because her eyes narrowed and her voice became shrill, "Don't tell me she is doing the city a service. I want this woman behind bars. Shut down!"

When Thompson's voice raised enough that I could make out what he was saying, Kelly flinched. "Wiles and your daughter just brought down a serial killer, I'm not about to arrest her and you should be thrilled to have a daughter as brave as yours. If there is any kind of danger, I can assure you that your daughter is in good hands."

"But that's just it—" Kelly tried to start again but then frowned and looked at her phone. Her gaze turned to me with a look of disbelief, "He hung up on me."

I shrugged trying not to look like the cat who caught the canary. "What can I say? The police aren't that reliable."

Kelly shoved her phone back into her bag and glowered, "This isn't over."

"I wouldn't expect so," I called after her as she stomped across the stained carpet and to the door.

I followed behind her. I closed and locked the door once more and rubbed my face. I had jobs to do today but they were going to have to wait until after I'd showered and eaten. The way the day was going already, my clients were lucky I was even going to work today.

An hour and one quick meal of leftover Chinese later and I was at my desk. I tapped on the keyboard pulling up the calendar Trisha had set up for me. I needed something easy today. Something that wouldn't take a lot of brain power.

There was a guy looking for his lost dog who wanted me to help hunt it down. That couldn't be too hard. Right?

I wrote down the contact information and grabbed my jacket and shoulder holster. It was just a simple job; I probably wouldn't need the gun but I felt better with it on.

I stalked across the waiting room and headed for the door. Glancing down at the piece of paper in my hand, I turned the knob and opened the door only to find Sid standing there with his hand poised in the air about to knock. A hand that had a new rosary wrapped around it.

"Uh, hey," he licked his lips and dropped his hand, tucking it into his pocket. Rocking back on his heels, he glanced down at my jacket and the paper in my hand, "Are you going somewhere?"

Cocking my head to the side, I took him in and realized I wasn't the only one who'd had a rough night. So, instead of giving him crap about being at my door, I said, "Yeah, to look for a dog. Want to come?"

Sid gave me a lopsided grin, "Sure, I've got some time."

16

I WAS ACTUALLY THANKFUL Sid had shown up. Though things were still a bit shaky between us, I didn't own a car and with Trisha's mom going crazy, it probably wasn't a good idea to give my assistant a call.

"So? Where to?" Sid asked as he put his truck into drive.

I looked down at the paper in my hand and rattled it off. Sid frowned.

"Are you sure?"

"Yeah, that's what Trisha put down," my brow scrunched down in confusion, "Why? What's wrong with it?"

Sid shrugged before pulling away from the curb. "Nothing, just it's not a good neighborhood. Lots of demons hang out in that area. If there's a missing dog, then it's likely not still alive."

I stared out the window. I didn't need to ask him how he knew there were a lot of demons in that area, but it still bugged me. He'd shown me exactly what kind of demon he was last night, and it had left an impression. Not a bad one, but not a good one either.

If anything, I was impressed Sid was able to keep his demon side under such tight control. The rosary around his hand must have some crazy powerful holy powers. Just thinking of the aura of Sid's demon made me shudder.

"Hey," Sid said, reaching out and taking my hand. I hated myself for it but I flinched. He dropped my hand and gripped the steering wheel tight. "And here I thought we were making progress."

"We were...I mean we are," I began, and then sighed, "Can you blame me though? It's hard to go from the-guy-I-like-lied-to-me to the whole he's-one-of-the-things-I-hate-most, not to mention his-demon-is-really-scary and then back to everything-is-all-okay all in the span of a few hours."

Sid smirked and shot me a look, "The guy you like, huh?"

I glared at him and clicked my tongue, "Out of all I said, that's the part you choose to focus on?"

He chuckled at my threatening glare, "What can I say? I'm a simple guy. The guy you like."

I blew out a hard breath, "I'm not going to live that down, now am I?"

His gaze turned soft and he reached for me again, but hesitated. This time, I grabbed his hand in mine and squeezed it.

We rode like that with our hands joined, his thumb making small circles on my skin. I couldn't help but make a contented sigh. I'd never just sat with someone and held their hand before. It was kind of...nice.

"Mary," Sid said eventually, "about what happened in the office before."

"What about it? You weren't yourself. Forget about it," I brushed it off with a small smile.

"Not that time."

My brows furrowed at his words. If he wasn't talking about him going full-demon mode on me, then what was he talking about?

And then it dawned on me.

My face grew hot and my eyes darted down to our joined hands. He was talking about that time we had kissed—when he had awakened something inside of me that I hadn't even known I possessed. Thinking about it caused something to stir within me and settle heavy between my thighs.

"Mary, please," his voice was strained and my eyes jerked up to meet his darkened gaze, "You have to control your thoughts. It makes it harder," he let go of my hand, the other one tightening into a fist around his rosary.

My eyes widened. "You can tell when I'm..." I trailed off, unable to say the words.

"Yes," he nodded, his gaze darted to me and then lower to where that heavy feeling was. His eyes on me only caused the heat to intensify and I gasped.

Horns honked as Sid suddenly veered off the road and into an empty parking lot. I held onto the side of the door until he threw us into park. Lips parted, I turned to ask him what the heck that was about, then clamped my mouth shut.

Breathing heavily, Sid's eyes locked on me. There was a predatory gleam in them that caused me to press my thighs together.

I licked my lips, "Sid? Are you okay?" I asked, my voice a bit deeper than usual.

I watched as he swallowed thickly, like a man starving and I was exactly what he wanted to eat. After a moment, he closed his eyes tight and breathed in through his nose, a low growl resonating through the car.

"Sidney," I tried again. "Should I get out?"

"No!" he snapped, his eyes meeting mine, "Don't move. Don't run. Just think of something else."

"What's wrong with you?" I asked, my hand on the door-handle not quite giving up on the option to take off.

"The demon...inside of me," Sid strained to say, "the rosary helps keep it at bay, but I have to keep it satisfied or it will overwhelm me...like last night."

"What do you mean satisfied?" I dropped the veil to see inside of his soul. Usually, Sid's soul was white with a bit of murky edges nothing abnormal, but last night it had been pitch black. Now, it was beginning to darken again.

"What do you think, Mary?" he growled a bit forcefully, "Who's my father?"

His father, Asmodeus, was the demon of lust. That meant Sidney probably needed the same thing his father did. Sex. I swallowed thickly before turning to him again.

"Just tell me what you want me to do?" I offered, reaching a hand out to touch him.

He jerked back from me and snarled, "Don't touch me! And don't ask me that."

"Ask you what?" I kept my hands firmly to myself.

"The demon side..." Sid laughed, "Oh he really likes you, Mary. And offering yourself up to me like that...?" he paused and locked his eyes on mine, "He is eager to have you beneath us."

I swallowed hard at his words. My brain finally seemed to figure out what Sid meant. Just like vampires had to feed on blood—and Adara had told me some even fed on fear—Sid, like his father, fed on lust.

"Is that why your bar is so..." I trailed off, my voice falling quiet.

"Exactly," he shook his head, "I'm usually better than this. I swear. The bar

205

keeps him at bay for the most part, but after last night I haven't had a chance to..."

"Feed him?" I provided.

Sid shot me a bitter grin, "Precisely."

We sat there for a moment, the air in the truck's cab thick around us. The tingle between my thighs had lessened slightly but it was hard to get rid of the feeling completely. When the person you cared for-and was most attracted to—was having a breakdown because they wanted to jump your bones, it was hard to not be affected.

Chancing a look at him again, I was relieved to see that he seemed to have calmed down a bit, his knuckles less tight. But his breathing was still heavy and his eyelids still hooded as if at any moment he could freak out again.

"I have a job to get to, and we can't keep pulling over every time I get aroused," I smirked, "if you hadn't noticed, my body can't seem to control its hormones around you. So how do you...you know satisfy him?" I gestured at Sid as if the demon were there.

Sid chuckled darkly and then slid his tongue across the line of his teeth. "Don't ask me that, angel."

I slid across the seat of the truck until I was next to him and before he could stop me I grabbed his face in my hands.

"Mary," he warned.

I ignored him. "Look, you're in pain. In need. You've helped me plenty of times. This time it's my turn to help you. So please," I let go of his face and sank into the seat next to him. "Tell me what I can do to help."

Sighing in frustration, Sid finally ground out something I couldn't make out.

"What was that?" I asked, leaning closer to try and hear what he said.

"I need a release, alright?" he looked out the window and I could swear there was a faint blush on his cheeks. Instead of teasing him about it, I said, "Alright."

"Alright?" Sid's eyes turned to mine suddenly and I smiled.

"Yes. You keep forgetting, I'm not human," I shrugged a shoulder, "I don't have the same kind of stigmas on intercourse. In heaven, we don't even have sex for pleasure. We are assigned a mate

207

when it is time to make more brainwashed minions for God's army."

Then why do you want to go back?

I pushed the thought aside and before Sid could answer, I started to undo his pants. When his hands caught mine, I paused and gave him a confused look. "You said you need release, right? The easiest way to get a male to orgasm is by stimulating the penis," I glanced down at his lap where he still had my hands in his, "I, myself, have never caused a man to orgasm, but I'm willing to give it a go."

Sid chuckled, "I'm afraid it doesn't work that way, angel. Though, I might take you up on that offer at a different time."

I cocked my head to the side and asked, "Would you prefer oral? I've heard that is particularly pleasant as well," I tried to undo his pants once more, but his hands tightened on mine again.

"If it was that easy, don't you think I would have been jerking off this whole time?" he raised a brow at me, "I wouldn't even need the bar to feed him."

"Okay," I drew out, not quite getting what he was saying.

Sid leaned in close to me until his face was close to mine. "It's not my release I need, Mary. It's yours."

Jerking back from him, I frowned. The feeling between my thighs pulsated and Sid closed his eyes tightly before giving me a wolfish grin.

"I've never done that," I exhaled, not sure why I was suddenly breathless. Giving Sid pleasure was one thing, but when I was the one of the receiving end, I was a bit unsure.

"There's a first time for everything," Sid said trying to reach for me. But I backed away.

"I mean, I don't even know if I can do that," I shook my head at him, "I'm an angel. Not a human. If we were programmed the same way, I'm sure the rest of my kind would have been going at it the way you do down here."

Sid reached for me again, an eager determination on his face, "Believe me, angel. If a half-demon like me can, you most certainly can. And will."

Clearly he saw my uncertainty about being able to provide him with a release as a challenge. One that he seemed set on conquering.

I tried to swallow and found my mouth dry, my throat strangely parched. I licked my lips, but it didn't help. "Okay. What should I do? Should I take my clothes off?"

Something in Sid's eyes grew eager, but he shook his head and glanced around us, "No, we are in too public an area for that. But maybe..." his eyes flickered to my pants, "Yeah, if you just take your pants off, it will be easier."

Hands going to the button of my pants, I suddenly felt shy about disrobing in front of him. I didn't know what it was about him, but Sid made me feel more human than anyone I knew. Which was why I should stay as far away from him as possible.

I ignored my warning and pulled my pants down my legs. It was a bit awkward in the vehicle but I got them off. Sitting there in only my underwear and t-shirt made my skin ache. Was this anticipation for what was to come?

"Now what?" I glanced up at Sid whose eyes were trained on my bare thighs.

Sid's glanced up from my lap to my face and then back down again. "It's up to you. I just need a release near me, I don't have to be the one giving it."

Chewing on my lip, I stared at the dashboard. He was giving me the option of not having him touch me. But the part of me that had been on fire ever since we had started holding hand didn't like that idea at all. Besides, I wouldn't know the first thing about giving myself an orgasm. If I could even have one.

"I think," I started turning back to Sid, "I think I need you to help me."

Before I could even finish getting the words out, Sid had me up and in his lap, my butt pressed against the edge of the steering wheel.

Sid didn't say anything, just cupped my face with his hands and then pressed his lips to mine. Only being the second kiss I had ever experienced, I had to say this one was very different than the last. Firstly, because I was half undressed in his lap, secondly because there was a sort of desperation in the way Sid's mouth moved over mine. As if he had been waiting for much longer than this to taste me.

My hands sat on his shoulders as I let him direct the kiss. His tongue stroking mine and then his teeth nipped at my lips. While I enjoyed kissing him, I was beginning to wonder how he expected to get a release like this, but before I could voice my concern his hands were on my hips. And then they were urging me to move.

Giving in to his direction, I allowed my hips to move back and forth across him causing the junction of my thighs to rub against the part where I assumed his cock was. I'd seen plenty of penises in books and on some of those shows Trisha had shown me, but I'd never felt one like this. Not pressed against me and making zings of something run through me.

What was that? Like little jolts of electrical current were running through my veins from where we were pressed against each other. It made my skin buzz and a startled noise come out of my throat.

Pulling away from the kiss, I stared down at Sid in confusion and wonder, "What's that?"

Sid smirked up at me and made my hips move a bit faster causing an even louder noise to come out of me, "That, angel, is the beginnings of an orgasm."

With my breathing heavy and my eyelids hooded, I only nodded and kept moving my hips in the delicious pace he had set.

It didn't take long before something large built inside of me. "Oh," I gasped my fingers digging into Sid's shoulders making him wince. I let go of him so I didn't accidentally hurt him, and instead placed my hands on the window a little bit behind his seat.

"That's it, angel," he whispered encouragingly, "Just like that. You're almost there."

How he knew how far along I was I could only credit to his demon half. I, on the other hand, didn't know what the hell was happening. The large ball of tension that had begun to tighten almost painfully between my thighs suddenly unraveled causing my hands to bang hard against the glass, shattering it as I cried out.

A shudder ran through my body and then a sort of euphoria that I had never experience before settled in. Trying to catch my breath, I leaned my forehead against Sid's. "So that was..." I couldn't get the rest of the words out before I started to laugh.

"An orgasm?" Sid provided with a satisfied grin on his face, "Yes. The first of many I hope."

I opened my mouth to answer him when there was a knock on the driver-side window. Our attention jerked toward the noise to see, Detective Riley standing there.

Sid rolled down the window as I slid from his lap and grabbed for my pants.

Riley's eyes were glued to my bare thighs as I pulled my pants up over my hips. "Looks like you know Mr. Magnus quite a bit more than you let on, now don't you, Ms. Wiles?"

17

DETECTIVE RILEY STOOD OUTSIDE of the driver's side door, a self-satisfied look on his face.

Even with my pants back on, Riley kept leering at my legs as if I was still undressed. I scowled at him and crossed my legs. I opened my mouth to snap at him but Sid beat me to it.

"What can I help you with, detective?" Sid leaned forward trying to block the Riley's view of me.

"What happened to your window?" the detective asked, avoiding Sid's question.

"A rock."

"A brick," I answered at the same time as Sid. Shooting him a warning look, I frowned, "Some kid threw a rock-like brick and broke the window. We were on our way to get it fixed."

"Really?" the detective rubbed his chin and then smirked. "'Cause I could have sworn I saw you, Wiles, break it just a few minutes ago."

Damn. This was why I didn't lie. Too easy to get caught in it, and even harder to get out of it.

"You know you're pretty strong for a woman," Riley's gaze went from the window to me.

"I work out," my jaw clenched painfully. I wasn't about to tell him.

My answer seemed to amuse him because his eyes snapped to Sid and he smirked. "Tell me, Magnus. Is she as good as they say?"

"What do you mean?" I couldn't help but ask.

"Oh, you know," a wicked grin covered Riley's mouth, "There's no way you'd have the sergeant wrapped around your finger so well without a little... exchange. And I'd say..." he licked his lips and leered at me, "...I'd be happy to get in on that action."

I saw Sid's hand tighten and I grabbed his fist before he could hit the detective. Sid's eyes shot to mine and I shook my head. No need to get him arrested for hitting an officer, even if the bastard deserved it.

"What are you doing here, detective?" I sighed, not bothering to correct his lewd accusations. He would think what he wanted whether I denied it or not.

This time he didn't change the subject. His eyes hardened and his lips thinned. "It seems like your pussy must be magic because not only is the sergeant in your pocket, but some Hollywood hotshots. They have the police acting like your personal delivery service."

I didn't even need to ask him who he was talking about. There was only one Hollywood hotshot that I knew and he was currently being possessed by the demon of lust.

Sid had tensed up beside me and I had a feeling he wasn't expecting such a visit either.

"So what are you delivering?" I asked. Riley dug into his coat pocket and pulled out a white envelope. Sid snatched it from his hands with a glare and then handed it over to me.

I took the envelope from him. It was thin and lightweight. I ripped open the top of it and reached inside. My fingers brushed against something soft inside and I carefully removed it from its envelope.

A single feather but not just any old feather, it was an archangel's feather. More importantly, it was one of Ramiel's.

"Mary? What is it?" Sid reached over to touch me but I jerked away from him.

"Drive, now."

* * *

MY STOMACH CHURNED THE entire ride back to the office. When I had told Sid to drive he hadn't even questioned me and we'd left the detective yelling in the dust. I'd probably hear about it from Thompson later, but right now I couldn't think about that. The only thing on my mind was the feather clutched in my hand.

"So, are you going to tell me what happened? What's up with the feather?" Sid asked as we sped down the highway.

I'd been quiet up until now, my mind racing with too many thoughts. What the feather could mean? One reason was obvious. Asmodeus had found Ramiel. The question was, in what manner did he get the feather from my former commander. An archangel didn't just give up a feather for no reason. They were too precious to part with.

"The feather belongs to Ramiel," I stated, my gaze fixed forward.

Sid hummed and out of the corner of my eye he nodded. "So it's a message from my father."

"Yeah."

"So what are you going to do?" Sid asked as we pulled onto my street. I thought about what to say to him as he parked in front of my building. My mind was reeling. I didn't know what to do or say.

On the one hand, I couldn't leave Ramiel with Asmodeus. I could imagine what Asmodeus would do to him if I didn't bring him the blade. A flash of a dark memory—filled with screams and pain— made me wince. No, I couldn't leave

Ramiel with Asmodeus. Not if I could save him.

"Mary?" Sid asked again, and I shot him a look and then smirked, "What I always do...save the day."

I jumped out of Sid's truck before he could ask me anything else and started toward the stairs that led to my office. Before I could enter the building, Madame Serena stepped out of her shop.

"Mary! Just who I wanted to see," my landlord's eyes lit up when she saw Sid following me out of the car, "And who is this dashing young man? Seems I was right about you meeting a dark man," she gave me a knowing look before offering Sid her hand, "I'm Madame Serena, but you my dear can call me Kitty."

Kitty? I mouthed behind her back to Sid, forcing back the grin threatening to spread across my face.

Sid took it all in his stride and enveloped Madame Serena's hand within his, giving her one of his dazzling smiles, "Pleasure is all mine."

My grin widened and I stepped up before Madame Serena could offer to read his future. "We're actually in a hurry,

Serena. Was there something you needed?"

Her eyes turned from Sid, a kind of school girl like blush on her face. "Oh yes, dear. I was going to say if you are going to have visitors at all hours of the night, please make sure to purify your area because it makes the whole building stink of evil," she waved a hand at the building behind her, "I haven't had a single customer today because of it."

Nodding, I grabbed Sid and pulled him toward the stairs, "I apologize. I'll make sure to do a cleansing right away. Have a great night!"

We rushed away before Madame Serena could stop us again. The feather was still clasped in my other hand and as we raced up the stairs my smile fell. There were more important things to worry about than Madame Serena's interest in Sid.

Opening the door to the office I stopped in my tracks making Sid bump into my back.

"What is it, angel?" Sid asked, but my eyes were on the person sitting behind the reception desk.

Dressed in a long-sleeved black-and-red striped top, Trisha sat in her chair. Her face free and clear of her usual makeup, leaving her face bare and looking even more tired than usual. What really stuck out though was the black-and-blue string of marks around her neck. It made a fist of sadness clench around my heart.

"Mare," Trisha stood from her chair, her voice a bit scratchy.

"Trisha," I said, my voice trembling for some reason. While I had stood up to her mother and claimed Trisha would never leave, a part of me hadn't really believed it. Any smart person would have left a long time ago. Apparently, Trisha and I had that in common, "What are you doing here? Your mother was very clear that you weren't coming back."

Trisha didn't smile at me, or even acknowledge my question. Instead, her eyes went to the other side of the room. I followed her gaze and landed on our less than comfortable couch where Doctor Ryan sat.

The short man stood to his feet and adjusted his glasses, "Ms. Wiles, I've been trying to reach you."

222

My eyes narrowed on the doctor as I stepped further into the office, "One would think all the unreturned calls would be a hint."

Doctor Ryan frowned hard, "I could see how this might be something you wouldn't want to discuss, but you have to understand. I have a duty. I took an oath to protect and heal those in need. And I believe your blood," he stepped toward me, an eager look in his eyes, "...your DNA, could revolutionize the way we heal people. We could help so many people don't you see?"

When I didn't show the reaction he seemed to have hoped for, he turned his attention to Trisha and Sid, "Tell her. She could save so many lives just by allowing me to run a few tests. A few vials of blood and that's it."

"Don't look to me." Sid held his hands up. "I'm on her side."

"You need to leave." To my surprise, this came from Trisha. Her eyes were hard, and her hands clenched into fists.

"You are obviously too young to grasp the importance of this situation."

"No. She's right. You need to leave. I can't help you," I gestured toward the door.

"You aren't getting what I'm saying at all," Doctor Ryan shook his head, his eyes were filled with a new kind of determination. The kind that showed he wasn't playing nice anymore, "People like you are what is wrong with this world. There is so much sickness, so much despair, and you could ease some of that suffering. Don't you have a soul beneath that hard exterior?"

"Sorry. Can't say that I do," A smile tipped my lips and I exchanged a look with Trisha who also grinned.

"Look here, you bitch," Doctor Ryan grabbed me by the arm, his teeth clenched, "I won't have you making a mockery of me. If you will help me, whether you want to or not."

Sid stepped forward to intervene but I shook my head. My hand went to my gun and I glared down at his hand on my arm. "Let me go. And get the hell out of my office."

Doctor Ryan hesitated when his gaze went to my gun. His hand dropped from

224

my arm and he adjusted his coat with a huff, "This isn't over."

He stalked out of the room and I called after him, "Thanks for thinking of Wiles Investigations!"

"Mary!" Trisha chastised though she was laughing.

"What?" I shrugged, "I have a business to run. Which reminds me," I crossed the room and wrapped Trisha in a tight hug.

"Mary, you're squashing me," Trisha croaked, though her arms came around me, returning my hug.

I pulled back and let out a big sigh, "I'm so happy to see you." My fingers came up to touch the brushes at the side of her neck. "I'm so sorry Trisha. I said I'd protect you, and I failed again."

Trisha shook her head, "No, no. It's not your fault, Mare. You can't protect me from everything. And I knew what I was getting into by taking this job."

"Still...maybe your mother is right," I ran a hand through my hair and glanced over at Sid and then back to Trisha, "Maybe you should find another job. One with fewer chances of dying."

"No way!" Trisha cried out, "I'm not going anywhere. Besides, who's going to make sure you don't turn to the dark side if I'm not around to keep you grounded?"

We shared a grin that Sid interrupted by clearing his throat, "While this is all heartwarming and whatnot, isn't there a more pressing matter?" his gaze shot down to my fingers which still clutched Ramiel's feather.

I held my hand out and opened it so that Trisha could see it.

"Is that what I think it is?" she grabbed my hand, but didn't take the feather from me.

"Yeah," I nodded and exchanged a look with Sid, "Problem is, how do I save Ramiel without giving Asmodeus exactly what he wants?"

"Wait," Sid said, putting a hand up, "You're not planning to hold up your end of the deal, are you? You know that's suicide, right?"

I placed my hands on my hips and scowled, "I can't exactly let a demon lord cross over to our plane. He causes enough chaos possessing people."

Sid shook his head, "You're crazy. You've met my father. If you don't follow through on your side, then he won't only hurt you. He'll hurt your friend Ramiel as well," he pointed to the feather in my hand.

"I have to try. I can't let—" I started to speak but was cut off when my the door burst open, revealing Adara with Madame Serena in tow.

Adara's dark eyes took in Trisha and Sid before she turned to me with a grin. "Looks like the gang's all here. What'd I miss?"

18

MY EYES DARTED TO Madame Serena and then back to Adara. "Uh...Adara. What is she doing here and better yet, what are you doing here?"

Adara grinned and nodded to Madame Serena, "Serena here is the guild's resident Wiccan."

"Wait, what?"

My mouth dropped open as I stared at the woman who had been my landlord for the last few years.

"Don't look so surprised," Madame Serena huffed, "I might play the part of a flighty wannabe but that doesn't mean I really am."

"But you can't even predict the weather right," Trisha asked and I nodded in agreement, "How could you be working with them?"

Adara stepped in this time, "Serena is one of the most powerful Wiccans we have in the city. I'm ashamed of you, Mary. You of all people should know that appearances don't mean everything."

"Besides," Madame Serena continued, "if every Tom, Dick, and Harry knew that I was the real deal, I would have them beating down my door wanting a love spell for this, or a charm for that," she crossed her arms making her bangles clang, and sniffed, "I wouldn't have time to do my real job."

"And that is?" I cocked a brow.

"Watching over you, of course," Madame Serena gave me a once over, "You get into more scraps than a rodeo clown," she shook her head, disappointment on her face, "you'd think an angel would know better."

"Wait. You know what she is?" Sid asked the worry on his face not unfounded. "What about...?"

"You?" Madame Serena gave him a nod. "Of course, but like our friend Adara here..." the older woman saddled up next to Sid with a flirty grin, "I don't have a problem with demons. Especially, ones with these kind of muscles." Madame Serena stroked a hand up and down Sid's arm causing him to tense and Adara to snicker.

I pointed an accusing finger at the ex-hunter. "You put her up to this, didn't you?"

Adara chuckled, "Of course, I did. Do you think I was really going to let you go out on your own with no backup? Do you really think the guild would have let you go out on your own?"

"I thought they didn't know about me."

The ex-hunter scoffed, "No one can wipe their asses in this town without the guild knowing about it. That's how I found out you needed me."

The thought of the guild watching me didn't sit well. I didn't like to be on anyone's leash, let alone people I didn't even know. I'd had enough of that in heaven. And while I trusted Adara with my life, I knew how self-focused the guild was and I didn't believe for a moment that they had my interests at heart. They'd take me out the moment I became a nuisance to them.

"So, what did you hear?" Sid spoke up, asking what I was just about to.

Adara turned to the half-demon with a serious expression, "I heard your daddy has been making friends and finding lost archangels," she shot me a raised brow, "I even know that they sent you a message in a form of a feather from said angel."

I opened my hand to reveal the feather. Adara and Madame Serena took a half step forward, their attention trained on the white object in my hand. I had seen the expression in their eyes in many humans before. Even Trisha had looked at Ramiel's feather the same way.

An angel's feather was a high sought-after commodity. It would fetch a pretty penny on the black market, if you knew who to sell it to. Even better, it could make some of the best spells more powerful. I could imagine that's what Madame Serena was thinking.

I closed my fingers around the feather and lowered my arm to my side. Adara and Madame Serena's expressions became neutral.

"So, did you bring me the blade?" I asked, my eyes going to the wrapped package in her hand.

"I sure did," she brought the bundle up and unwrapped it, displaying the blade.

"How'd you know I was going to give it to him? Maybe I was just going to let him rot after what you told me," I asked, my eyes on the blade. This thing could save Ramiel. But it could also doom the rest of the world.

"'Cause I know you, Mary," Adara flipped the blade over and offered me the hilt, "You would do anything to save Ramiel, even if it meant letting a demon through to this side."

I shot a glance at Sid out of the corner of my eye. He was avoiding my gaze, but his face was hard and I could tell that Adara's words bothered him. I wanted to assure him that I still cared for him, but now wasn't the time. I didn't know how long I had until Asmodeus decided to start taking pieces off Ramiel and sending them to me like he'd done with the feather.

"Alright," I said, taking the blade by the hilt, "So you delivered the blade, but I still don't know what Madame Serena is doing here. Did you just want to gloat that you've been watching me, or what?"

"Not at all," the psychic said, and then stepped toward me, "I'm here to help you get that demon through to our side, but with a little hitch."

"What do you mean? Help me? I'm just delivering the blade and grabbing Ramiel. That's it," I shook my head.

"That's the other part I'm here for," Adara's face grew dark, "Your dear friend, Asmodeus, didn't tell you the whole deal, and I'm sure he'll be happy to fill you in as soon as you get there, but I thought it best you know beforehand. That blade," she gestured to the dagger in my hands, "it can make a portal to hell, sure, but it can't be used by just anyone. Only an angel can use it. An archangel."

She stared at me for a moment as my mouth dropped open. I mean, it kind of made sense. It was Michael's blade after all. God wouldn't allow just anyone to use it. But what I wanted to know was why Asmodeus had even sent Sid after it in the first place if he couldn't use it without the help of an archangel.

"Sid?" I turned to him, but he looked as confused as the rest of us.

"Don't look at me like that, angel," he shook his head, "My father makes me do his bidding sure, but I'm hardly in the inner circle. I'm just as in the dark as you are."

I believed him. When Detective Riley had shown up with the feather he had seemed as surprised as I was. It wouldn't be unusual for Asmodeus to not share his plans with his son. Sid was, after all, mainly on my side. Or at least, I hoped he was.

I stared at Sid for a moment longer and then turned to Madame Serena, "So what's this hitch?"

The psychic's lips curled up into a wicked grin, "Oh, you are going to love this," she pulled out a necklace with a star charm that looked suspiciously like it was made of some kind of animal bone. Maybe a chicken?

"What's that?" Trisha asked, coming closer to take a look.

"This is what will give you the upper hand," Madame Serena held it up so that everyone could see.

"So I wear this thing and then what?" I asked, "Blast him with some kind of power?"

"Oh, no no," Madame Serena shook her head, "This isn't for you. This is for Asmodeus," she smiled, a giddy gleam in her eyes, "Your job is to get it around his neck once he gets over to this side."

"But what does it do?" I reached out to touch the charm and felt a weird buzzing go through me.

"Think of it like a stopper," Adara offered, a shit-eating grin on her face, "He might be flesh and blood on this side, but he can't use his powers as long as that thing is around his neck."

"So, you're neutering him!" Trisha said with a grin.

"I guess you could say that," Adara nodded, "With this on, he won't be able to harm even a fly."

I frowned and stared at the charm. It sounded too good to be true. "But what's stopping him from taking it off?"

"That's the best part," Madame Serena let out a giggle, "Only the person who put it on can take it off. So, you just have to make sure to never take it off him."

Well, that was easy enough. I wasn't planning on doing that anytime soon. Especially since—if he finds out what I did to him—Asmodeus would come at me full force. I just had to make sure I was ready for it when he did.

"Alright. Sounds like a plan," I took the necklace from Madame Serena and tucked it into my pocket, "Now, we just need to figure out where Asmodeus is keeping Ramiel."

Everyone in the room turned to Sid who sighed and took out his phone, "Fine. Give me a minute."

* * *

It didn't take long for Sid to find out where his dad was holing up at. Asmodeus had changed venues on us and for once was staying at one of the many five-star hotels in Los Angeles.

"At least it's not another warehouse," Trisha said as we drove down the road.

"You could have stayed at home you know," I countered, "I don't want you to get hurt."

Trisha shot me a grin, "Don't worry, I'm going to stay safely in the car until you come running out of the building. Think of me as the getaway man."

"Just make sure you stay out of sight," I pointed at her and then swiveled around and faced Sid in the backseat, "Are you sure you want to do this? You'll be telling your dad which side you're really on."

Sid nodded and offered me a grim smile, "I've never been on his side. But I have been too cowardly to say so right out. But if your plan works, I won't have to worry about him anymore."

"If it works," I reminded him, I tapped Michael's blade held in a sheath on my thigh. "The moment I use this baby to open the portal, we have to get that necklace around his neck. If not," I shook my head sadly, "you'll be putting a target on your back."

"Angel," Sid leaned forward and cupped my cheek with his hand. "If there's anyone's side I want to be on, it's yours. Target or no."

"Aw, you guys," Trisha cooed and sniffed, "You are making me want to cry."

I turned back in my seat as we pulled up at the hotel, "Well, save it for when we get out of this thing alive."

Trisha pulled around back so that she wasn't in plain sight of the entrance, but didn't kill the engine, "Okay, so the moment you come running out of there, we're out of here. No pit stops for a victory make-out session," she shook a finger at me and Sid.

I grinned at her and ruffled her hair, earning me a growl, "This shouldn't take long. Lock the doors and keep your eyes peeled."

"You got it boss angel," she gave me a two-finger salute as Sid and I climbed out of the car.

As we approached the front door, two guys—who were obviously part of Asmodeus's group—stepped out of the shadows. Sid grabbed my hand and gave it a squeeze. "Are you ready for this?"

I smirked at him and unclipped my Glock, "As I ever will be."

19

I DIDN'T GET A chance to pull my gun from its holster because the demon goons held their hands up in front of them.

"We don't want any trouble, angel," the bigger of the two stated. He had light hair and intelligent eyes, even if the guy he had picked to possess had a seventies fashion sense. "Walter and I just supposed to take you to the master once you arrived."

"Oh? So he was expecting me? That makes me feel so much better," I scoffed.

Walter, who was a paunchy short fellow, scowled and took a step forward, "Listen here you bitch, you will lick the feet that Asmodeus, the great demon king, walks on. You are not worthy to even be in his presence."

"So, he's a demon king now?" I shot a grin at Sid who simply shrugged, "I'll have to make sure to pay my respects to His Majesty before I put a bullet through his head for threatening my friend."

Walter's face started to redden but his companion placed a hand on his chest, stopping him from doing anything else. "It's alright, let her say what she wants. She'll change her tune once she's in front of the master."

This made Walter grin, an amused look covering his face as he chuckled, "That's right. We'll see who's laughing when you're before true evil."

I forced back the urge to roll my eyes as the two demons led Sid and me into the hotel. We passed by the check-in station where a brunette teenager hid behind the counter but one glance at her and I knew she was possessed as well.

"Geez, we're surrounded," I mouthed to Sid.

"What did you expect?" he responded with a grim expression, "To just waltz in, do the deed and get out in under five minutes?"

"No," I pouted, "but an angel can dream."

"This way," Walter's companion took us to a set of elevators where they were ready and waiting for us to board.

"After you," Walter snickered and gave me a mock bow.

"I don't think so," I shook my head, holding my ground.

"Come on, Mary," Sid took a hold of my elbow, "They're just minions. They can't do anything to us or they'll get in trouble."

"He's right," the larger one said, "We are under strict instructions to bring you to the master, and that is all. If we lay one hand on you, he will kill us."

"Ah," Walter whined, "Why'd you have to go and tell them that. I was having fun."

"Because," Walter's companion shot a look to his companion, "I would prefer not to get shot because you can't control your mouth." He then turned to us, "Please, get in. The master is waiting on the top floor. We will not be going with you."

I eyed the two demons for a moment and then cautiously stepped into the elevator. When they didn't follow us, I relaxed a fraction. I pushed the button for the top floor and watched the doors close. The last thing I saw of the demons was the smaller one flipping us off, and it made me smiled.

"You guys sure are colorful, I'll give you that," I said, glancing at Sid who gave me a hard look.

"Don't put me with them. They are nothing but bottom-feeder hell-scum." The rage in his voice made me flinch.

"Sorry, I didn't mean to offend you. I know you are nothing like those guys," I glanced down at the ground.

"Do you really, angel?" There was genuine uncertainty in his voice that made me reach out to take his hand.

"Of course, I do. I might have thought so before but I won't make that mistake again. There might be great evil living inside of you, but there's also good there," I pressed my other hand to his chest feeling his heart beat beneath my palm, "That doesn't just make you better than other demons but most humans."

"Thank you," Sid laid his forehead against mine, "you don't know how much it means to me to hear you say that."

"Well, don't get used to it. You'll get a big head," the elevator dinged and the doors opened to the top floor.

242

We stepped out of the elevator and right into a large room. There were a few demons scattered around the edges, standing with their backs to the walls of the circular room. In the center of the area were a few couches arranged in a circle around a prone figure on the ground.

"Ramiel!" I cried out, rushing toward the crumbled form of my former commander. Sid tried to grab me but I shook him off.

Ramiel was still breathing but he was decorated in cuts and bruises. Dried blood covered the side of his face making his auburn hair turn slightly darker. His body clothed in tattered garments and one glaring fact shone out. His wings. They were gone.

"Do you like my handiwork?" Asmodeus's voice rang out from the left side of the room. My eyes darted to where he stood, shirtless and in a pair of lounge pants. His hair was wet, as if he had just taken a shower but even with his good looks he only made me sick to my stomach.

"This wasn't part of the deal," I said between clenched teeth.

Asmodeus simply smiled and strolled across the room, "Now, what kind of example would I be for my fellow demons if I just handed him over to you without getting my pound of flesh?"

Surging to my feet, my anger pulsing through my veins, I grabbed the dagger from my thigh sheath, "Here's what you asked for, now take so we can go."

The demon lord looked to the other demons lined along the room's walls and they shared a laugh. They thought I wasn't in on their plan, but thanks to Adara I wasn't the butt of this joke.

Not that they needed to know that.

"What's so funny?" I asked, glaring at Asmodeus.

"Finding your friend was a bit more difficult than I had previously thought, and took more resources out of me and so it's going to cost you more than just delivering me the dagger," he smiled at me as if he thought he had me where he wanted.

"What else could you possibly want?" I growled, my patience wearing thin.

Instead of answering me, Asmodeus looked behind me to where Sid stood.

"Sidney, how nice of you to take an active role in this. I hadn't expected you to hand-deliver her to me. I will have to be sure to find some kind of reward for you later. Maybe you'd like to play with her some before I kill her?" he licked his lips as he leered down at me, leaving no doubt what he was thinking.

"I'd appreciate it, father," I glanced behind me to see Sid offer his father a lopsided grin before giving me a heated look, "She's been a rather difficult one to break."

I had trusted Sid when he had said he was on my side, and even now I still believed him. But he played his part for his father almost too well. It almost made me believe he had fooled me from the beginning.

Almost.

"So that was the plan all along?" I complained, "Have me to get your stupid blade, then kill me? What was the point of even finding Ramiel for me, then?"

"Well, we have to have an archangel to perform the ceremony after all," Asmodeus smiled, "and what better motivation than to save your precious friend."

"Why would I do that? You are just going to kill us both anyways."

"Now, that wouldn't be very wise on your part," Asmodeus taunted, coming closer to me, "You see. I might end up killing you after this little get-together, but there's nothing keeping me from going after your little friend. What was her name?" he pretended to think about it for a moment.

"You keep Trisha out of this," I snarled, slashing the dagger at him, Asmodeus jumped back and waved a finger at me.

"Now, now. Play nice and we can all get out of here alive."

Though already aware of his plans, I was becoming frustrated. The longer we stayed there the more chances that something was going to go wrong.

"You just told Sid you were going to kill me. Would you make up your mind already?" I huffed.

"A demon can change his mind," Asmodeus shrugged.

"Fine. Then let's just get this over with," I stepped over Ramiel and walked over to Asmodeus.

"Let's do this by the window," Asmodeus ushered me over to the floor-to-ceiling windows, "Isn't this view spectacular?"

The view was stunning. The whole city was lit up and even the Hollywood sign was visible from here. Definitely worth the five-star rating in my book.

"Sure," I grunted.

Asmodeus's brows scrunched down for a moment as if trying to figure me out, but then he shook his suspicion off with a grin, "I'm sure you know how to use a blade, but just to be certain, let me show you."

He stepped aside to gesture at one of the window panes, giving me no choice but to watch him.

"You should grip it with your whole fist and slash in a downward motion," he demonstrated with an empty hand, "Think of it like you would be ripping through a curtain."

I frowned and pretended to concentrate on the window before me, "And then what?"

"And then my dear, I come through to this side and you get to take your little friend home with you." The grin on his face was that of a liar. There was no way he was letting me leave. With or without Ramiel. But he didn't know I had my own ace up my sleeve. Madame Serena's charm burned a hole where it sat in my pocket and I forced myself not to bring attention to it.

"Should I do it now?" I asked.

"Whenever you are ready," he offered me a small smile, as if I were a child needing encouragement.

I wasted no time in gripping the hilt of the blade in my fist and doing exactly as he had asked. I expected the blade to hit the glass, but it caught on something invisible and as I pulled it down a light flashed out of the hole I was creating.

"That's it," Asmodeus urged me on, "Just a bit more."

I pulled the knife down until I'd carved a gap in the nothing in front of me. When I stepped back, I looked to Asmodeus but he was lying on the ground. Or rather the body of the actor he had possessed was.

My eyes shot back to the gap I had created and I watched as a hand came out of the light. It wasn't clawed or gruesome-looking, it was actually a pretty normal human hand. It gripped the side of the hole and then another hand came out and grabbed the other side.

I tucked the blade back into my thigh sheath and dug into my pocket for the charm Madame Serena had given me. The moment his head popped through I was going to loop it around his neck and then bolt.

A mop of dark hair—followed by a head—began to emerge from the light but before I could even raise my hand to put the charm on him, I was tackled from behind.

I fought against my attacker, the charm clutched in my hand. When I was able to roll over, I wasn't surprised to see the shorter demon from the lobby.

"You," I growled, "I should have shot you when I had the chance."

"You should have," the demon laughed as he struggled to keep me down. "Now, I get to tear you apart for my master."

"You're not supposed to touch me remember?" I reminded him, lashing out and punching him in the face.

He let go of me long enough for me to search out Sid, who was standing before the portal where his father now stood in flesh and blood.

My mouth dropped open. The man standing there was the spitting image of Sid. If I didn't know any better, I would say they were twins. In fact, if Asmodeus hadn't been buck naked and steaming, I'd have sworn they were.

"Sidney!" I cried out. When his eyes shot to mine I chucked the necklace at him.

He caught it and before his father could figure out what was going on, looped it around Asmodeus's neck. Immediately, the demon lord's face contorted in anger. Which meant it was time to go.

My demon attacker was still on top of me. I grabbed the dagger from my leg and shoved it into his stomach. He screamed and rolled of me, clutching his bleeding belly.

Jumping to my feet, I pulled the dagger free and raced toward Ramiel. The demons who had been watching the show snapped out of their stupor and came at me. I pulled my gun from its holster and started shooting. I wasn't aiming for kill shots. Getting them out of my way would be enough.

I got to Ramiel and awkwardly dragged him over my shoulders. With my gun in one hand, I shot at the demons who just keep getting up. I was glad I'd refilled my magazine recently, or I'd have been screwed.

Sid met me at the elevator door with Asmodeus hot on his tail. "Go, go!"

With Ramiel's weight on my back, I didn't need to be told twice. As soon as the door opened, I threw myself in and pushed the button for the bottom floor. Sid raced after me but was jerked back.

"Where do you think you are going, son?" Asmodeus snarled, his hand on Sid's shirt. I didn't even think about it as I aimed for Asmodeus's chest. The shot rang out as Sid fell forward and the demon lord screamed.

The elevator doors closed, but not before I saw Asmodeus glaring at us, the hole I had made in his chest healing before my very eyes.

"So, I guess that charm doesn't stop all his powers," I commented, breathing heavily.

"It stopped him from killing us on the spot. That's a win to me," Sid smiled as he sat on the floor of the elevator at my feet.

When the door opened, Sid got to his feet and helped me carry Ramiel through the lobby and passed the desk clerk who was smart enough to stay where she was.

Trisha's car was still parked where we had left it except I could see through the back window Trisha singing and dancing in her seat. I opened the rear door on the driver's side and was blasted with one of the pop songs that Trisha had always talked crap about.

"I wasn't listening to that, I swear!" Trisha cried out, shutting the music off as a blush covered her face.

I shoved Ramiel in the back and climbed in after him while Sid got in on the other side. "We'll talk about your choice in music later. Drive."

20

RAMIEL WAS OUT FOR three days. During that time, he rested on my bed with me at his side, cleaning his wounds and generally just waiting for him to wake up and tell me where hell he'd been the last five years.

I hadn't heard from Asmodeus since I had left him at the hotel. But I wasn't getting complacent. He was going to try to get back at me for virtually neutering him. It was only a matter of time.

Until then I intended to watch my back and Trisha. Adara could take care of herself and Sid, well Sid was still his father's precious boy, even if he had helped us trick Asmodeus.

I had given Adara Michael's blade back and told her to make the guild put it in a safe somewhere the demons could never find it. I'd take it back to heaven with me if I ever got there, but until then it would be safe with them.

"How is he?" Trisha asked me on the third day, her eyes on the prone form.

I stood from the chair I had pulled up next to him and motioned for her to go out into the waiting area. Closing my office door slightly, I crossed my arms over my chest and shrugged, "As good as one could be after being tortured by demons."

Even as the words came out of my mouth my chest tightened. When I had been tortured it had left me broken and wild. Only Adara's tender care had been able to pull me out of it. I didn't know what kind of shape Ramiel would be in when he woke up. He had only been with Asmodeus for a little while, but any amount of time under the thumb of a demon was too long in my book.

"Do you think he'll wake up?" Trisha frowned, worry etching her face.

"I hope so," I chewed on my lip, dropping my arms to my side, "If he doesn't, I'm not sure what else I can do. There's never been an angel — archangel or not — being in a coma."

Trisha nodded thoughtfully and then asked, "And how are you holding up? You don't look like you've slept a wink. Have you even showered?"

"That's because I haven't done either," I gave her a weak smile, "Too worried he'll wake up when I'm passed out."

Curling her lip up in disgust, Trisha held her nose, "Well, you reek. I'm surprised he hasn't woken up just from the smell of you," she gave me a little shove, "You won't be any good to him if you can't stay awake. Why don't you let me watch him for a little bit and you go shower, eat, and get some sleep on the couch? I know it's not comfortable but..."

I placed a hand on Trisha's shoulder, "Thanks, Trish. I don't know what I'd do without you."

"Probably spend less time watching anime," she grinned at me. I went to hug her but she held her hand up, "No way. Shower first, then hugs. I'm not getting your demon funk on me," she shook her head and pointed in the general direction of my bathroom.

"Fine," I dropped my arm and headed back into the office with Trisha on my tail,

255

"You'll tell me the minute he wakes up right?" I glanced down at Ramiel, worry eating at me.

"The very second he peeks open his gorgeous eyes," Trisha flopped down in the chair I had been using and then did a shooing motion, "Go. Go before we all die of your gastric fumes."

"I don't smell that bad," I lifted my arm and gave a whiff before promptly dropping it with a cough, "Okay, maybe I do. I'll be right back."

I hurried into the bathroom and turned the shower on. Disrobing, I thought of the angel lying in my bed. I had spent all this time with only a sliver of hope that Ramiel was still alive, and now that he was and at my side I wasn't sure what was going to happen next.

I stepped under the spray and let the water wash over me. Without even soaping up I felt ten times better. I rubbed the loofah over my body scrubbing extra in a few particular spots. When I got to my back I paused. For the first time, I reached back and touched the scars on my back without flinching.

Ramiel's wings had been taken, just like me. We were a matching pair, he and I. Mine, I knew were probably mounted up on some demon's wall in hell. But Ramiel's? I had no clue where they were, or if we could get them back. Or if he even wanted to get them back. For all I knew, he might want to stay on earth.

Sighing deeply, I finished washing and got out of the shower. These were all questions that I could ask him when he woke up. If he woke up.

I toweled off and quickly dressed before making my way back into the office. While drying my hair with a towel, my eyes immediately went to where Ramiel was lying—in the same exact place as I had left him a few minutes before.

Trisha looked up from typing away on her cell phone and smiled, "There's my girl. I knew you were somewhere under all that dirt and grime."

I grinned back at her and tossed the towel I had used to dry my hair at her. The towel hit her in the face and she cried out, "Hey!"

"That's what you get for making fun of me," I grabbed the only other chair in my

257

office and pulled it up beside her, "How is he?"

"You mean since you were out here five minutes ago?" Trisha cocked a brow and then when I didn't smile she sighed, "Fine. He hasn't changed. Still passed out. Still lovely as ever."

My gaze went to Ramiel's sleeping form. Trisha's description wasn't off by much. I hadn't really paid much mind to what the archangel looked like before. He had always been pleasing to the eye but now that I had been on earth and knew what made someone attractive or not, Ramiel should have made that tingle inside of me flare to life.

His auburn hair was tousled and brushed the nape of his neck. I knew beneath those eyelids were dazzling blue eyes that had never hesitated to smile at me. While all angels were in shape, high metabolism and no need to really eat, Ramiel seemed to have gained more muscles in his biceps and chest. Overall, he was on the higher end of Trisha's drool-worthy scale.

You'd think just the sight of him would excite me, the way it was with Sid. But for some reason, I didn't get that same urge to embrace him. I didn't have an overwhelming need to be close to him. I cared for him, yes. But did I want to be with him the same way that I had been with Sid?

Not really.

Was there something more to Sid that caused my body to react in such a way? Or was it just him in general? I had always thought Ramiel would be the one I would eventually mate with, but as I gazed down at him now, I couldn't envision it.

Sighing, I stood from the chair, "I'm going to grab something Chinese from downstairs. Do you want anything?"

"Nah, I'm good," Trisha waved me off, her eyes locked on her phone once more.

"Alright, I'll be back in a few minutes. Call me if he wakes up before then."

"Will do," Trisha offered me a thumbs up, not looking up from her phone.

Frowning and shaking my head, I started toward the door. Before I got through it a distinctively male groan stopped me. I spun on my heel, my eyes darting to the bed.

Ramiel rolled over on the bed and then adjusted himself once more. I rushed to the side of the bed and dropped to my knees.

"Ramiel?" my voice was shaky and so full of hope that it I feared I might cry. Which was silly. I never cried.

My commanding officer rolled around on the bed again until he was turned toward me. I glanced over him to Trisha. Her eyes were wide and her phone hung limply in her hands, whatever she had been doing forgotten.

My attention moved back to Ramiel who grimaced but then muttered, "Muriel."

"Yes, it's me. I'm here," I grabbed his hand in mine and squeezed it. Then I frowned. While sitting by his bedside, I hadn't really thought about holding his hand. I'd only been worried about waking him up. But holding it now, it was different. Strange even. It wasn't like I hadn't ever held his hand before. I had, in heaven. But it had not felt like this.

Before I would always get a kind of feeling of relief and contentment. Like I was finally home. Now though, holding his hand felt heavy and made me a bit sick to my stomach.

I didn't have much time to think about it because at that moment Ramiel's eyes fluttered open. The bluest of blues locked onto mine and I felt...nothing. Absolutely nothing.

"Muriel," Ramiel said once more, his brows lifting in surprise. He let go of my hand and reached out to touch my face, "Are you real?"

I forced back the feeling of revulsion that had swept through me at his touch and smiled, "Yes, it's really me. You're safe now."

"I thought I was going to die."

"You almost did," Trisha spoke up from the other side of the bed. Ramiel tried to roll over to see her but cried out as soon as his back hit the bed.

"Hey, hold on a moment," I said placing a hand on his shoulder to stop him from moving, "You're still healing."

Trisha's eyes went to Ramiel's back and her nose crinkled, "Yea, your back looks wicked bad, dude. You shouldn't move so much."

"It does?" Ramiel's eyes widened and he tried to reach behind him and touch the wounds on his back.

"Don't touch it. It'll only make it hurt worse," I chastised, grabbing his hand. "When did you lose your wings?"

Ramiel's brow furrowed and then he shook his head, "I...I don't remember. I had them before...the demons!" Ramiel shot up from the bed and then cried out and fell back down.

"The demons are gone now. I took care of them," I eased him back onto his side.

"You did?" he looked me over as if seeing me for the first time. "Muriel, what's happened to you? You've changed."

"Well, it's been a long five years," I shrugged a shoulder.

I wasn't surprised that I looked different. Five years on earth would do that to an angel. Last time Ramiel had seen me, I had worn the basic white garb of our kind with gold plated armor over my chest and stomach. Matching braces used to cover my arms and shins. Where that outfit had gone, who knew. It was probably still in hell with the rest of my innocence.

"And you've been here this whole time?" Ramiel asked, looking to Trisha who had moved around the bed to my side.

"Yeah, pretty much. Except for a short bit in the beginning when I was still getting my bearings." I didn't mention to him that I had been recovering from my injuries I received from getting captured. There was plenty of time to catch up on those kind of things. Right now, it was about getting him well.

"What have you been this whole time?" Trisha asked and I shot her a warning look.

"Trisha! Now is not the time to be grilling him. He can tell us when he's ready."

"No, no," Ramiel placed a hand on mine, "It's alright. You have a right to know."

I frowned but didn't protest as he took a deep breath in and then told us his story.

"As you know, I came down from heaven to check on a report that some demons had gotten through to the human realm. Well, they had been right but there had been too many for me to stop on my own and I had planned to come back to get reinforcements but I wasn't quiet enough,"

Ramiel's gaze grew dark as he spoke, "The demons caught me and took me to hell with them. I don't know how long I was down there. I don't remember much of what happened either."

He shook his head, and the lost look in his eyes made my chest tighten.

"I just remember waking up by the side of the road near the city. I walked for while until I came across a house," he paused for a moment, as if he didn't want to say the next part, "I have to admit I did some things I'm not proud of. Stole something clothing from a clothes line. And a few other things."

I gave his hand a reassuring squeeze, "We all do things we have to just to survive. No one would blame you."

Ramiel returned my smile with a weak one, "Anyway, I got to town and I spent the next few months trying to learn the human world. It wasn't until a month ago that I heard about you going to the hospital in the news."

"That was on the news?" I exchanged a look with Trisha who shrugged.

"Yea," Ramiel chuckled slightly and then grimaced, "I thought it was a sign from God that he hadn't forgotten me."

"But then why didn't you stay when you sent the flowers? Why just disappear like that?" I couldn't help the hurt in my voice.

"I didn't know if you wanted to see me. Besides, you had enough people around you to take care of you," his gaze went to Trisha and softened, "I knew you'd find me when you got out and you did."

"Well, technically, a demon did," I corrected him.

"Yes," Ramiel's voice hardened and his gaze locked with mine, "We will have to talk about why you are consorting with the enemy later. Right now, I'm tired and starving."

Guilt ate at me, but I pushed it down and stood from my chair. "I was just about to get something for us to eat. So why don't you rest for a little while longer and I'll bring you some too."

Ramiel nodded, "Sounds good."

He turned slowly from his side until he was on his other side, his back to me. Now that he was cleaned up and I was able to actually pay attention to his wounds they made me frown.

I gestured for Trisha to follow me as I made my way out of the bedroom. I moved to the other side of the reception area and kept my voice low.

"Somethings wrong."

Trisha's brow furrowed. "What do you mean? He's awake and seems to be as lost as you were. Shouldn't you be happy?"

I shook my head, my mouth in a thin line, "His story sounds plausible but it doesn't add up. If he had been taken by demons like I had, he would have lost his wings five years ago."

"Maybe they weren't as crazy as your captors," Trisha offered up with a shrug.

"What about how he was able to blend in with the humans on his own?" I asked and then kept going, "Or how he just woke up on the side of the road?"

"What are you getting at, Mare?"

"The portal I came out of was in the middle of nowhere and I was in no shape to get through the forest, let alone get to a road. It was only cause Adara found me that I was about to get better."

"Okay, so maybe his portal came out somewhere else."

A darkness filled me as I remembered how I was when I'd finally escaped. "You don't escape hell with your mind intact, Trisha. If he had gotten out he wouldn't have been sane, let alone together enough to find clothing. I was like a rabid dog, ready to attack anything that came into my path. The story he tells doesn't portray that."

"Maybe he just didn't want you to think less of him," Trisha looked back toward my office door, "If he was as animalistic as you say, then I don't blame him. I wouldn't want anyone else know either."

"Maybe," I drew out.

"Anyways," Trisha clapped me on the shoulder, "We'll figure it out. We always do. Now let's go get some food. All this drama is making me hungry."

I followed Trisha out of the office and down the stairs. What she said made some sense, but I didn't tell her the main reason I was suspicious.

The scars on Ramiel's back. They were still fresh, as if his wings had been taken just minutes ago. If his wings had been

267

taken when he had been captured either time, his body would have healed by now. It would have adapted to the change, covered them up like they were never there.

But Ramiel's wasn't like that. The bones of his wings still protruded from his back. They weren't white as they should be, but blackened and burned. There was only one way an angel's back would look like that after their wings were removed. One reason that made my stomach twist and knot in denial.

Ramiel had fallen.

DECEIVED BY HELL

Everything seems to be going Mary's way now that she has love in her life. A great job, no demon possessions in sight. But things go sour when she realizes the person she knew has secrets of their own.

With every new development pointing to betrayal, Mary will be damned if she let hell stand in her way of being happy. Hell hath no fury like an angel scorned.

ABOUT THE AUTHOR

Erin Bedford is a *USA Today* bestselling fantasy and paranormal romance author, a computer programmer by day, and a hobby hoarder.

Creating fantastical worlds have always been a secret passion of hers and she couldn't imagine writing any story without some kind of lovey-dovey or smexy goodness in it.

Read More from Erin Bedford
erinbedford.com

PREY BY NIGHT

Bill Williams works for the Marquesa running contraband from Tangiers to the Spanish Coast. That is, until the Association decides to scuttle his boat one dark night, almost killing him and his mate Paco. Williams knows he has to fight back just to stay alive, but who and where is the Association? How do you find an enemy who operates even further outside the law than he does? Things become further complicated when Paco finds out that Williams has been seeing his sister, Maria, and feels he must protect her honor. And then there's Lavinia Hatherton, a rich blonde with an expansive taste in men. And Blasco, a Spanish cop hot on a trail of blood. In a frantic night filled with assassins and temptations, Williams soon finds his greatest challenge is just to stay alive.

RAIN OF TERROR

Jake Abbott is a European reporter with a hell of an assignment. Piscoli is a small town in the Italian mountains south of Naples and it's being flooded by torrential rains. Ralph Ellison, Jake's boss, wants him to head up there and report back. Grace, Ralph's wife, wants Jake to stay with her. But Jake has got other problems. He has inadvertently humiliated a local crime boss, and now he's got Angelo on his tail with murder on his mind. And then there's Leverett, part of the committee assigned to assess the damage; Harry Myers, Jake's photographer; and Captain Luca, out for blood. They're all heading up the mountain as the rain pours down, cascades of mud and sudden floods washing by. It's a recipe for disaster, and that's just what happens when Ralph turns up dead in the flooding—and all evidence points to Jake as the killer!